I0747918

M. AINIHI

Resist

A Blood Inheritance Novel

This book is dedicated to you,
my wonderful readers.
Thank you.

Contents

Prologue: Consequences

The Chaos Realm

Amanda sucked in a breath and eyed her surroundings, trying to get her bearings. She had ended up on a dirt path. Yellow and green shrubs lined either side. It appeared that her dark magic had brought her back to the Chaos realm, just as she had intended.

She turned in a slow circle until her eyes locked on to the water's edge, where the stone bridge reached up to stretch across the familiar lakelet, with its impossibly perfect half-circle arch. Only now the steepest point at the center of the construct was missing, and what remained looked more like two arms reaching up for something, anything to hold on to.

A knot grew in her stomach, and she released a low groan as she thought of how the ground had shaken with the weight of the rock monster just before she had used her gem to aid in a hasty retreat. Amanda cast her gaze below the bridge, but the murky water reflected nothing back.

The knot in her stomach tightened as she remembered how awestruck she had been by this place on her previous visit before the infuriated creature had attacked.

She drew her eyes toward the opposite bank, hoping to catch sight of the vibrant red and orange grass that had stood in patches near the shore, casting a fiery illusion against the once clear surface. But from this distance, the thin blades looked shriveled and dark.

Amanda clenched her fists. She had caused this.

Ashamed, she sank to her knees and closed her eyes. As she did, the image of the crumbling bridge was replaced by a vision of the ruined mountain she had just fled from.

She knew the celestial's prisoners had wanted her to do it, to sacrifice them, and in the end she had because they made her feel she had been given no other alternative, and when that hadn't worked, they had manipulated her until she wanted to do it.

Amanda let out a groan as she whispered, trying to convince herself that it was true, "There's always a choice."

She wanted to believe it, although deep down she no longer did.

She reached her arms across her stomach as it twisted painfully with the fresh memory, but the alien feel of her regenerated limb against her natural skin only increased her discomfort.

Denied a few moments respite and reminded of why she had chosen to look for answers in this realm, she opened her eyes and pushed herself back up to her feet.

She pivoted away from the ruined bridge and headed farther down the path she had arrived on before more unpleasant memories of her time in the mountain could invade her mind.

1

Emily - Tension

The Human Realm

Emily breathed in deeply. She had made up her mind. She was going to show Kiami the letter she took from the castle. The letter Amanda had written, seemingly to herself, so long ago. She needed to. Yet her legs felt like cement, even as her brain and heart urged her to move on. She lifted her eyes back to the words on the page and reexamined them.

Am I a hero or a villain?

I was just a girl trying to do the right thing ... at least that's how I recall it, but as the days go by, I can't help but ask. This question has been gnawing at me for some time, and as the search for my mother continues to come up empty, the hole in my heart continues to grow, not because we haven't found her, but because I am not sure I want to. The truth is I am afraid of what I will find if I meet her.

If the jinn could grant wishes, as they did in human myth, I would turn back time.

That hit home with Emily, and she read on, refreshing her memory.

But they can't, and nothing I do will bring back the things I have lost. I want to forget about the choices I have had to make since I first encountered Erol's artifact in the woods, and the things the sorcerer stole from me when he dragged me into his fiendish plot. I only knew that if his evil was allowed to grow, he would not only destroy us but also everything that is wonderful about the world. Is it really better to sacrifice the few to save the many, and in making that choice, did I condemn myself to a lifetime of darkness?

Out of necessity, I attempted to embrace the shadow magic that I inherited from my mother, but it is stronger than me, and I can feel it growing day by day with every move I make. I fear it will take over by the time I am through.

I searched these books, trying to find a way to save us all from Jacob...

The name caused Emily to shudder, and she tore her eyes from the page as an understanding of her reluctance settled in.

Amanda had only relieved the once powerful sorcerer of his magic.

Days ago, Emily's own encounter with him had ended his life.

Goosebumps erupted on her arms at the thought. She dreaded reliving the experience, but she would if she needed to. Emily closed her eyes and sucked in a deep, calming breath. She was stronger than this. And right now, she needed to focus on Kiami.

Whatever Kiami had been through with Amanda on the mountain had left her visibly shaken. She could only hope that the note would help to restore some semblance of her usual optimism before Justin could notice the difference in her demeanor. When she had returned from the mountaintop, she seemed unconnected, shaken, barely a reflection of her naturally cheery self.

Emily took another deep breath, then glanced down at the page as she refolded it to present to Kiami.

Kiami was still sitting in the sunchair where Emily had left her as she approached. "Don't lose faith. We have to hold on to what and whom we believe in. I need to show you something." Emily thrust the note at her and waited while she read it silently.

When she was done, Kiami turned her face away as she spoke softly. "It seems unreal now. It feels like a mirage. Everything that happened on the mountain, everything I saw."

Emily felt a small lump growing in her throat. She cleared it before responding. "We will never know for sure what is going on in Amanda's head all the time, and that's okay. This note shows you that she is who you thought she was, doesn't it?"

Kiami sat up straighter, and Emily saw movement from the corner of her eye. She snatched up the note and stuffed it into her pocket just as she heard Justin greet them.

She leaned down and whispered into Kiami's ear, "When everything around you goes bad, you can't always be good."

As she pulled herself back, Emily couldn't help but notice that Kiami's face seemed to visibly redden, and for a moment it tensed, causing deep lines to appear across her forehead, then just as suddenly, her face went slack again.

Emily shot her a questioning look, and Kiami responded by lifting the bag she had been clutching in her lap as she whispered, "It's not just the circumstances around the collapse. There's more. A lot more."

Emily glanced over her shoulder at Justin, then pointed in his direction before she spoke again, but this time loud enough for him to hear, "We have some things to tell you too. Why don't you get some more rest while we fill you in?"

Kiami gave a slow nod of understanding as she lowered the bag back into her lap, just as he bounded up the steps with a sheepish smile plastered on his face.

Emily realized she wasn't the only one relieved to see Kiami. She casually folded her arms in front of herself and grinned back at him. "I suppose you would like to start with the amulets?"

He gave a quick nod, then, as if an explanation was warranted, he said, "They were my idea, after all. And in the order of events..."

Emily stepped backward to lean against the outer railing, trying to appear relaxed as she responded, "By all means. Regale her with tales of your heroic accomplishments."

His eyes seemed to twinkle with excitement as he looked at her. "Are you poking fun at me, Emily?"

"Maybe. Just a little. But seriously, have at it."

Justin wasted no time filling Kiami in on how he had hung amulets on the tree in an attempt to stop whatever magic was allowing the prying eyes to sprout on its branches. He didn't even seem to pause for breath as he went on to explain how the act had triggered the memory of the tree's history, which had seemed more relevant with each passing moment as he recited it anew for Kiami.

He began, "An updated but condensed retelling, if you will."

Then he rolled the wrist of his outstretched hand and gave a brief theatrical bow before starting. "Long, long ago, an Arcane sorcerer, whom we believe to have been Jacob, somehow made it to the Emerald Mountains, or jinn realm, if you prefer. While there he kidnapped one of the younglings, whom we surmise was none other than Aden."

He paused, lifting his eyebrows and widening his eyes as if shocked by the revelation, then continued.

"This caused panic amongst the inhabitants because many of the jinn believed that if one of the arcane sorcerers could make it into the Emerald Mountains, more would follow."

Again, he lifted his eyebrows and this time raised his hand to cover his mouth in a brief but silent dramatic show before returning to the tale.

"It was decided that they would go against their traditions and beliefs to protect their younglings by sending them to the human realm.

"Unfortunately, given their youth, not all the younglings had manifested the ability to travel in such a way, but some of the elders knew of a tree that was fabled to have roots so deep, they connected the Emerald Mountains to the human realm. They located the tree and used it as a conduit to force the youths through, whether they were willing or not."

Justin frowned at his own words, but his eyes twinkled with delight.

"Among this group of younglings was a jinni named Jaali who had witnessed the kidnapping first-hand. He desired to stay behind and fight back if more of the arcane showed up."

Emily watched as he took a step toward Kiami and bent down closer as he explained, "You see, besides being ripped from his home, he had lost two friends that day: the youngling that was kidnapped—"

"Aden?" Kiami asked.

"Yes, and the guardian that had been in charge of them, Erol."

He paused, looking expectantly at Kiami as if awaiting another response. Emily rolled her eyes at him and cleared her throat to get his attention before motioning for him to continue.

Justin straightened up, scrunched his face up at her, then began again.

"Jaali tried to bury his wrath inside and vowed to seek retribution when he could. But his ill intent started to manifest on the outside, and as he took on more and more of the characteristics of an Ifrit, the jinn from the town tried to intervene. They wanted to help him quell his anger by finally sending him back to the Emerald Mountains with one of the elders."

Justin started speaking faster. "Then, one morning, the townspeople woke to find the conduit tree burning and the elder that had accompanied Jaali unconscious in the grass nearby."

He began to pace back and forth between her and Kiami. "They raced to put the fire out, but the tree had been engulfed in flames. They would have thought it was dead if they couldn't still feel magic emanating from it. They dug down into the ground until they found the point at the roots where the fire had not damaged them. Then, with the aid of a spell, they covered the tree in a layer of stone to help preserve it as best they could."

Justin stood still and slowed his speech. "Later, when the elder came to, he told the townspeople that they had found their village in the Emerald Mountains almost abandoned. Only a few jinn had not moved on. This affected Jaali in a way he hadn't predicted. Jaali confessed to the elder that the kidnapping had been his fault.

"You see, Erol was being inattentive that day because the council was deciding if he had earned the right to visit the human realm for the first time. Which was a big deal for jinn, but Jaali was fond of him and afraid if he left, he would never return. So he encouraged the younglings to misbehave. Being a youngling himself and inexperienced with the feeling of the sorcerer's alien magic, he had led the flock of younglings toward the stranger.

"So, feeling as if it was justified, Jaali had pleaded with them to release Erol and imprison him instead. But it was the guardian that had failed in his responsibility to protect Aden, and magical imprisonment isn't that easily reversed."

His excitement seemed to lessen, and his words became quieter.

"Deciding that Jaali's ideas were bad for everyone there, the elder and the remaining jinn from the Emerald Mountains tried to force him to return once more to the human realm with the aid of the ancient tree, and that's when he and the tree burst into flames."

Kiami clapped her hands. "Great storytelling."

His eyes seemed to sparkle with the compliment. "My pleasure."

Kiami sat up straighter in her chair. "So, the tree is still alive?"

"Very much so," Justin replied.

"And it can be used to help get to the Emerald Mountains?"

"So the legend goes. Why?" he questioned.

Kiami shrugged then look down at her hands in her lap. "Just curious, I guess."

"There is one more thing, Kiami." Justin bent forward and took her hand. "I have to apologize to you for the way I have been acting. I told Emily, and I am telling you now, I will try my best to do better."

"There is no need to apologize. No one expects you to be complacent. None of us will ever be the same as we were when all this began."

Emily looked away from the pair, drawing her eyes toward the street. She had been happy to hear Justin repeat the apology he had given her to their friend. But Kiami's response caused her to feel a pang of guilt. She was right.

As Kiami continued, she seemed lighter. Like the weight of worry had been eased from her shoulders. And sounding much more like her old self, she smiled as she addressed Justin again. "I am happy that you realize you were being foolish. Mostly."

Although she was glad to see that Kiami seemed cheerier since Justin's tale unfolded, she couldn't help but wonder what exactly had caused her spirits to finally lift.

Justin cocked his head to the side and smirked. "Mostly?"

Kiami pushed herself up from the chair. "I should never have followed Amanda to the mountain."

His smile wavered, and real concern crept into his voice. "What happened up there, Kiami?"

"I put myself in danger."

"From Amanda?"

"No. I ... she saved me. I got stuck mid-transformation."

Justin's face grew pale as he exclaimed, "That sounds awful."

Emily couldn't stop her own imagination from conjuring up an image of Kiami, lingering somewhere between human and bird form, and she shuddered.

Kiami looked down at her feet as she added, "It's not something I would ever want to repeat, that's for sure." She turned her gaze back up at Emily and expertly changed the subject. "The amulets you spoke of are working well to stop the prying eyes? You guys have been checking the tree every day?"

Emily was a bit thrown off by the sudden change of subject. "Well, Justin has been, and it seems like they are doing what he intended. For now, at least. Right?"

She glanced up at Justin, and he nodded as he added, "So far, so good."

Kiami let out a sigh as if relieved by his words. "Anyway, back to what I was saying before. On the mountain, Amanda and I got separated. That's when the wisps showed up, and I met Blaine."

"Who?" Justin asked, confused.

"I'm sorry if my thoughts seem scattered," she said as she sat back down in the chair. "I just don't want to leave out anything that seems..." she paused as if in thought, "important right now," she finished.

Curious about where this was going, Emily listened quietly. Kiami had not mentioned Blaine earlier.

The excitement had crept back into Justin's voice as he addressed Kiami. "So, did the wisps lead Blaine to you?" He glanced over at Emily. "Like they led you to the camera..."

Kiami shook her head. "That's not what I meant. Blaine *is* the wisps."

Justin lifted his hand to push the dark hair back from his face and revealed a doubtful expression. "The wisps are a single being?"

Kiami sat up straighter and used her free hand to motion at each of them. "Like us."

Emily struggled to remember exactly what they had pieced together about their heritage. They were all only half human; their other genetic parentage, one of a magical being, gave them abilities human beings didn't possess.

Emily shifted her weight back to her feet. "A half-blood. Half human and half something else?"

Kiami gave a quick nod before adding, "He can send pieces of himself to different places at the same time."

Justin's expression slackened. "That explains some things. Like how the wisps would know to post a photo of the house we were staying in to help Etzion find his way to us."

Emily was anxious. She didn't want to spread her worry, but she couldn't stop herself from asking, "Why hasn't this being shown himself to us?"

"I think it's good news; it means that there is only one more like us to find. Bloise confirmed that there were seven in total. One half-blood for each realm. Me, you, Kiami, Amanda, Etzion, Blaine, meaning our jobs are almost done!" Justin said excitedly.

"You mean that *part* of the job is almost done, don't you? Anyway, I'm just being cautious. Remember how Aeron tried to trick us into thinking he and Etzion were both like us, when in fact he was trying to use Etzion against us?"

"We remember, Em," Kiami answered then explained, "Blaine was trying to stay under the radar, but I think that is going to change soon. I think once Blaine knows it's safer here, he might show up."

When she stopped speaking, she rocked back in her chair with a satisfied look on her face.

"But is it really safer here?" Emily looked down at her hands and started wringing them together.

"Come on, Em. We stopped the eyes, didn't we?" Justin said with an air of confidence, adding, "It is great news."

It was, she thought, but she had made up her mind that she had something to share with Kiami as well. She turned to her and belted out the words, "Jacob showed up too." Then she dropped her hands back at her sides in resignation. She felt like a hypocrite saying so after having asked Kiami to keep the fact that Amanda may have been the person to bring the mountain down herself, but she scolded him anyway. "Why keep it from her?"

Justin raised his hand toward her. "Stop." His gleeful expression was quickly replaced with a stern one as he continued, "You let him have what he wanted. He won't be back. Leave the subject at that."

"Why not tell her about your latest wisp encounter instead."

As he tried to push her recent interaction with Jacob out of the spotlight, Emily's cheeks burned. She crossed her arms over her chest as she added, "I just think Kiami needs to know that it hasn't been all sunshine and rainbows here. It's not always as safe as it may appear."

"It's all right, *Em.*" Kiami stressed the nickname as she reached forward and grasped her arm. "I know we need to go. Blaine told me you needed me to come back so we could move forward."

Emily looked to see her expression had changed. Her face had hardened, and her eyes seemed to search Emily's as she said, "But before we prepare for that, I want to show you one more thing."

2

Kiami - Fragments

The Human Realm

Kiami hoped she had made the right decision. It was the words that Emily had whispered to her that compelled her to mention Blaine. The being had told her to say something if the time seemed right, and Emily's words had been so similar to what Blaine had said about Amanda that once she found out the spying eyes were disabled, she gave in.

Justin at least seemed to gain some relief from the knowledge. Emily, on the other hand, seemed leery.

Perhaps, Kiami thought, *Emily just felt it was too good to be true. After all we have been through. Or wondered why I didn't mention Blaine the first time I told the story.*

She cleared her throat nervously. She did not like keeping things from them, and she still had not told either one that during her time alone with her on the mountain, Amanda had revealed she was the cause of her guardian Jacqueline's disappearance all along.

Kiami raised a finger to her mouth and chewed at her nail, reminding herself that some things needed to be left out, for now at least. Justin's tree legend had given her an idea of how she could reach Jacqueline, and Kiami hoped that when this was over, she would find her guardian still alive and waiting in the jinn realm, where Amanda had banished her.

Next, for Justin's sake, Kiami reiterated what had happened to her after the mountain fell. Only this time leaving out the fact that she had noticed evidence Amanda could have caused it. She swore she heard Emily breathe a sigh of relief as she finished the tale.

Kiami popped up from her chair and ushered the pair into the house, where she emptied the contents of her modified hood onto the table for them to inspect.

As they looked over the pieces, Kiami's thoughts kept drifting back to Jacqueline, her mother, and the stories they had told her about the mountain, Hara Berezaiti.

"And you found these pieces of metal around the ruined mountain?" Justin asked, interrupting her thoughts as he continued inspecting the objects.

She remembered how the glimmer of the half-buried items had caught her eye. "Well, I thought they were metal at first but now... Truth be told, I was distracted when I was collecting them."

Justin released the cylindrical piece he had been examining dropping it back onto the table, then folded his arms in front of him as he looked into her eyes, awaiting her explanation.

"Something was watching me."

"Blaine?"

She shook her head. "Something unfamiliar and dangerous. I couldn't pinpoint it, and the feeling just wouldn't go away. I panicked and fled. The entire way here, I couldn't shake it."

She looked back at him, thinking of how she had felt the first time she entered town and landed on the tree with the spying eyes.

"It just creeped me out. Maybe it was nothing, but I have learned it's best to trust my instincts in regards to such feelings."

Justin lowered his arms. "Maybe you were just reeling from the collapse of the mountain."

"So you think I was being hysterical? Do you remember the way that old wizard, Bloise, warned us away from following Amanda to begin with?" Kiami was careful to keep her tone even. She wasn't mad at his questioning, but she wanted to understand his thought process.

"Sometimes a piece of metal or plastic is just that. Maybe you are reaching for answers that are not there. The whole event sounded pretty traumatic; it would be understandable."

Kiami furrowed her brow. "Yeah, but these came from inside the mountain. A mountain that appeared to be nothing more than a natural landform, by all accounts... Don't they look like machine parts of some sort?"

"They could be." He pointed. "This one kind of looks like a clutch. I mean, I don't have much to go on." He moved his finger forward toward several twisted pieces that had dull teeth around the inner and outer edges. "Those could be broken gears."

Kiami spoke with enthusiasm. "In the myths my guardians taught me, that mountain was known as the watch post for the sky. It was said that all the stars revolved around that particular peak."

"How's that supposed to help?" Justin asked.

Emily shushed him. "What else did they say?"

"When I asked why they would choose that place over others for a watch post, my mother gave me a warning. She said I must remember that what makes something special is not always visible."

Emily offered, "What if the mountain was hiding something much bigger? Maybe something similar to the illusions that the old wizard Bloise had cast when we visited him ... but a much more complex one.

Perhaps if we went there and tried to find more pieces?"

Kiami's eyes went wide, and she looked up. "No."

"Well, we should do something, Kiami. We can't just stay in place. It would feel like giving up. Justin can wait here for Amanda if you want," Emily stated.

Kiami explained, "Blaine said I needed to get back here so that we could leave. But not back to the mountain. He said that we need to go with you to find the seventh."

"So, your guardians, Bloise, and Blaine all made the mountain seem unsafe?" Justin asked then added, "Did Blaine at least hint at where we should start?"

"Not exactly," Kiami said.

"Well, we better prepare anyway," Emily retorted.

"How do we know what to be ready for?" Justin inquired.

Kiami thought back to a time when Amanda had told her about how this all started and quipped, "Be ready for anything."

3

Amanda - Gardening Tips

The Chaos Realm

Every morning at daybreak, Amanda reminded herself that time passed differently in each realm. Just as she had aged more slowly during the period she spent in the Arcane territory than those she left behind in the human domain, here the opposite was rumored to be true.

She hoped it was. For her weeks had gone by since she first arrived in the Chaos realm as she watched, waited, and planned. And after all this time, the statues remained her only real clue as to the location of the goddesses, whom she believed were being held prisoner by the celestial.

Amanda thought of the image that had been painted in the room far below the bookstore. She remembered how Emily had insisted on showing her the secret place hidden behind the heavy door and how she had led her alone down the sloping passage that would bring them to the underground lair.

She wrinkled her nose at the memory of the smell, as if she was there now breathing in the aroma of incense and mothballs as they passed under the rounded stone doorway and into the room with the paintings. She closed her eyes and tried to recall small intricacies.

Within the landscape image, there had been two detailed gardens with a tree-lined footpath in between. The same footpath she stood on now.

Amanda had just come from the circular garden. She had been inspecting the topiary within it for changes, a task she completed almost daily since her arrival. She wasn't sure who did it and had long presumed the slight alterations to the topiary's expressions and details had to be getting made overnight. The rest of the garden was well maintained, flowers were sown, and weeds were plucked regularly, but even with as much time as she had spent there, she had never witnessed anyone tending those forms.

The designs had a human appearance, and the seven figures they represented very well could have been anybody, yet she felt herself drawn to them again and again.

Since the celestial had made a claim that the inhabitants of the Chaos realm created likenesses of them within their territory, she knew the pull she felt could have been no more than the product of his suggestion. Whether or not he had been lying, these were the only such effigies she had come across.

Today, a silver feather had somehow stuck itself atop one of the bushes, reminding her of Kiami and how they had parted. She had let the tears fall, remaining stationary, not even bothering to wipe them away.

Somehow, letting them make their own trail down her cheeks and land where they would felt necessary, and the inaction on her part offered a slight relief from her guilt at the way they had parted, her forcing Kiami to drop her into the river by owning up to the fact that it had been her that took her beloved guardian from her.

When the tears stopped, she reminded herself it had been the only way to stop Kiami from inflicting more pain on herself and keep her safe from the truth that had been hidden inside the mountain.

She turned toward the second garden and breathed in the aroma of the small, flowering trees within it. She wasn't supposed to enter, and she had only done so on one occasion, but she had managed to see much of it before she was made to leave.

To say it was filled with short, flowering trees didn't do it justice. Where one waist-high treetop stopped, the next began, making it hard to see the grass or dirt below them. The walkway that branched off from the path and into the garden followed the smooth walls of solid rock that enclosed three sides of the plot.

There were several square carvings near the bottom edge. Each of them had a crude face chiseled into it and stone-carved hands that were protruding just above the bottom of the square. The ground below them, where the grass would have grown upward covering the carvings, had been paved with small stones to form a semicircle.

She had only managed to see one of the carvings up close before she was ejected, and she longed for the opportunity to finish their examination, but today was not the day.

Amanda took in another breath, inhaling more of the aroma from the sweet-smelling flowers, then turned about to leave the gardens. She was behind schedule, and if she didn't keep up her prompt appearances, she would never be given the opportunity to fully explore the secrets she was sure the garden held.

4

Amanda - Fitting In

The Chaos Realm

Amanda had been escorted out of several places before she came to the realization that if she was going to get anywhere, she would need to learn to blend in. The rules hadn't been that hard to learn once she found the closest village and its library. It was finding where the humanoid inhabitants dwelled when they weren't near the gardens that had posed the first problem. The village itself was hidden with magic, in much the same way the jinn had concealed their own town in the human realm, but with what she thought of as a stronger recipe.

Here it was necessary not only to keep up their spells but also to use clever ruses in order to stop the plethora of dangerous creatures that lurked outside its walls from finding their way in, whereas the jinn village was spelled with the main purpose of keeping out non-magical humans or those that would mean them harm.

From the outside, the location would be made to look uninhabitable. When she left this morning, the solid stone walls around the village had appeared to be nothing more than a towering thicket of thorny bushes and brambles that not even a mouse could squeeze through. This ruse seemed to be their most frequent choice, and although the illusion changed based on perceived threats, it now appeared very similar to how she had discovered it the first time she entered.

After she managed to find her way in and began traversing the hidden village's ancient cobblestone paths, she discovered that it was her more human-like appearance that had the biggest potential to cause an uproar.

As a precaution, she kept most of herself covered with her cloak when she was inside and in the public eye. Although there were what she considered wide-ranging variations in the inhabitants' outward appearances, her own plainness would have given her away.

Thankfully, her rejuvenated appendage with its unnatural woody-looking texture helped to conceal the fact that she didn't belong in the Chaos realm at all, and she found herself displaying it often to dissuade questioning glances. Although she still hated it, and the memory of how she had obtained it consumed her at times, she had come to appreciate the unwanted gift.

Amanda scoffed as she remembered how she had tried to categorize the inhabitants' outward traits as plantlike, animalistic, insect-like, and so on. She had soon abandoned the task, realizing with two exceptions, one being those like the rodent-esque duo she was hurrying to meet, the process would have been like trying to categorize the many shapes of raindrops falling to the ground during a storm. The majority of those that were similar in appearance at first did not seem all that related on closer inspection.

Maybe, she thought, the two exceptions were proof that while Akila and Mia were in charge, they had tried to control the evolution of the realm's inhabitants. Control and manipulation did seem to be a favorite pastime of all the celestials on Sumir.

She paused and took in a deep breath as Jacqueline's words from her time as Amanda's captive reverberated in her head: "Into the seventh plane she threw her remaining ingredients at random."

She had been reciting a portion of the world creation myth that had been missing from the first version Amanda stumbled across. It was the explanation for how the goddess Sophia had created the Chaos realm and why it was given its name.

This seventh realm was meant to be her sister's prison from the start, after Akila and Mia had all but destroyed the humans. The goddess had been counting on nature to take up the reins in unpredictable ways, and it had not disappointed.

She clicked her tongue and started walking again, now thinking of the time she had spent here with Kiami, Emily, and Justin.

They had encountered a number of strange, beautiful, and dangerous creatures from the realm, yet their experiences hadn't quite prepared her for what she found within the walls of the village.

The fact was the life the humanoids led here was anything but chaotic. Their days were filled with tasks and rules to keep everything around them in balance, and to her it was clear that neither the celestial nor his daughters had much to do with it; rather, these balances were set in place long ago by the people themselves after they had been abandoned by the goddesses and before the celestial had inserted himself into their lives.

A time the villagers referred to as "The b'tween."

The distinction was even made in the library archives, although it had taken her some time to catch on to the fact that new chores and procedures had been altered or why. Once she had, the changes only helped to fortify her belief that the biggest clue to reaching the goddesses would be found within the garden that contained the crying fountains.

When she neared the place on the path that met the water's edge, two rat-like creatures that walked upright on their hind legs, similar to the ones that had helped URD in its attack of the castle in the Arcane realm, approached her with a brooch, a bag, and a rake.

"Thank you, Howin and Dhruv."

Although they didn't speak, they were masters at letting their feelings be known. The whiskers on their elongated faces twitched as they scrunched up their snouts at her in disapproval. She was late, and this pair appreciated punctuality above all else. Their prime directive was to make sure everyone got an assignment each day in a timely manner. It was an important job in a society where money did not exchange hands, and they were good at it.

"It won't happen again," she offered as she accepted her tools and handed them her eye-shaped brooch from the day before.

Other creatures like them could be found doing various odd jobs throughout the village. They were helpful by nature and would answer a call from those they liked without question. She was especially fond of these two. They were not sweet or loveable. To say they were would be a misguided statement, but their actions were honest, sometimes brutally so. She had seen up close on others the scars they could inflict with their claws and teeth if you crossed them or those they were loyal to.

She stepped away from the gruff pair and affixed the large beetle-shaped brooch to the shoulder of her cloak. The symbol represented your assignment, and today she was on reconditioning duty, due in part to her late arrival. Yesterday she had been given a much cleaner post keeping watch atop the wall, but she didn't mind the messy stable work; the chores allowed her a guaranteed meal in the evening, a place to sleep within the village walls, and plenty of time to think while she completed whichever mundane task she was given.

As she moved through the village and toward the stable area, the path beneath her feet vanished, and she marveled at the change in architecture. While most of the dwellings where humanoids slept and worked were made from natural stones of grays, blues, blacks, and light pinks, the housing for the animals had been created with fired clay bricks. The difference between the yellow facades in contrast to the stonework in the other areas always made it feel like she had entered an entirely different village.

When she approached the stable she was assigned to, she waved to the other volunteer within. His two lower teeth protruded as he paused his work to smile and nod at her before continuing to shovel manure into a wheelbarrow.

The only other exception she was sure of among the varied inhabitants, like the rodent-esque villagers Howin and Dhruv, the outward appearance of this citizen was the second recurring anomaly within the community.

During her first few days here, anytime she encountered someone like him who held similar qualities to the green-haired monster from her nightmares, Abaddon, she would have a hard time keeping dark thoughts from creeping in as the memories of him and Aedan would resurface. However, she was barely affected by the outward resemblances to him anymore.

Amanda hung her bag from one of the hooks at the entrance and began to rake up the matted hay within the first stall, letting her thoughts wander as she worked to recondition the space.

During her time with the celestial, he had claimed that the people of the Chaos realm didn't hate her and the other half-bloods because of the power they had to bring the barriers down. But given her encounters with URD and Abaddon, she had started her investigation believing that she would find nothing but animosity toward herself in this territory.

Ashamed, her cheeks burned at the memory of how going into this, she had expected to meet a bunch of monsters within the village. What she found was something else entirely, and she felt that she owed Emily a debt of gratitude for giving sound advice when she had warned them against making assumptions about the residents here.

The more familiar she became with the beings that lived within the village, the more she felt she had allowed herself to be misled, and she scolded herself for not inspecting the facts more closely all along.

The truth was, although Abaddon had seemed unnerved by her existence, URD had only claimed to be sent there by him and was following his directions. Jacqueline's distinction of him as the master of the realm of Chaos during her imprisonment had not been entirely inaccurate.

Though she didn't dare to tempt fate by bringing up the subject herself, through careful eavesdropping, which was often easiest to accomplish at mealtimes due to the cafeteria-style setup, she learned that people of this village referred to Abaddon as the self-proclaimed ruler, although she also learned he was given the title by a high authority that they would not question. The simple truth was that they were scared of him and this appointer.

Amanda could only assume that the authority was none other than the celestial, because they would not speak of him, but they would express relief at the fact that Abaddon had not returned in some time. Rumors that he had been vanquished spread, but it seemed how was an uncertainty they did not care to explore.

"I hear you came from a village far from here?"

She jumped at the sound of the voice that had broken her concentration and looked up to see the volunteer standing outside the stall with his hands firmly on the overflowing wheelbarrow's handles.

Choosing not to speak out loud, she nodded in his direction and sent him a half smile before turning back to her duties.

He let out a hearty laugh. "I heard you were quiet too." A low grunt escaped him as he hefted the handles upward. "Guess the rumors about that are true as well."

She paused in her raking again and lifted her face to address him, but he had already pushed his workload out the door.

Although she wasn't working as fast as she should be, she waited for him to return, and as he made his way past the stall, she addressed him following the village's local custom, raising her right hand as she spoke. "I be Amana."

The name she had chosen to use while she was here was close enough to her human name that she rarely neglected to answer to it. Likewise, on the rare occasion when she forgot herself and misspoke, the alteration was easily forgotten.

His eyes went wide as if she had caught him off guard, then he set the wheelbarrow down and copied her arm movement. "I be Bly."

"Well met, Bly," she responded then dropped her arm back to her side.

"Well met, Amana." He returned the pleasantry with a smile, then reached down for the handles again to resume his work.

When the last stall was complete, Amanda took a deep breath and mentally prepared for the heavy lifting of the next part of her job. As she walked back to the entrance of the stalls, she noted that someone had already started laying out the fresh hay for her in several of them. She looked around the stable, but it appeared that Bly had finished and taken his leave.

She approached her bag to retrieve the gloves and hay hook she knew would be inside. Instead, she found them lying in plain sight on the ground beneath it.

It wasn't unusual for the villagers to help each other complete their chores, yet to do so without acknowledging the fact or taking proper care of the tools loaned out was a new experience for her.

Amanda bent down to inspect them but saw no obvious signs of damage. She needed to finish laying the bedding in the remaining stalls before the livestock were brought back inside to escape the heat of the noon sun, so she shrugged it off as a fluke and then equipped them, assuming Bly had been in a rush after helping her.

By the time she finished carrying in the bales of hay and spreading them, she was sweaty and tired. Glad to be done with the day's tasks, she went to retrieve the bag from where it hung on the wall. When she lifted it, hard objects within rattled.

Amanda furrowed her brow and held the bag open in front of her. Inside, nestled at the bottom, were seven small pebbles. Each one was painted a different color.

No longer sure it was Bly that had handled her tools or her bag, Amanda's shoved the gloves and hay hook inside, then walked the length of the stable again as if inspecting her work, but she found no signs that anyone else besides her and Bly had been there.

Disconcerted, she intended to reevaluate the stalls one last time before taking her leave but relented as a fresh volunteer entered, tugging at the rope as one of the six-legged goat-like animals that were housed in this particular stable bounded in behind him.

5

Kiami - Security

The Human Realm

The idea that her guardians, Bloise, and Blaine had all been trying to warn her against visiting or staying near the mountaintop stuck in Kiami's head, and even as she should have been helping Emily and Justin to prepare to look for the other half-bloods, she found it hard to focus on the present moment.

She did want to contribute, but she was so restless she would find herself distractedly chewing at her nails when Emily would start asking her questions, or reorganizing furniture when Justin would suggest finding a useful piece of equipment to take with them.

She had managed to begin a search for flashlights when the cloth-bound book caught her eye. The first time she had seen it in her home when it fell from its hiding place, she was sure it held answers, but she had discounted the book after the pages went blank, thinking Bloise had done something to it in order to lead her and Amanda astray.

Now she wondered if she hadn't been wrong in the assumption, and she abandoned her original search as she retrieved the book. She ran her fingers over the light green cover before opening it to the first page, then stared at the flowing cursive name, "Rhiannon," in the top left-hand corner.

She flipped through the blank pages, thoughts of Bloise and her trip to the ruined mountain swirling. She turned back to her guardian's name, then snapped the otherwise empty book shut.

Kiami closed her eyes and tried to clear her mind. She had seen firsthand that the book contained writing and images, but the old wizard had been the one wielding it at the time.

Journals often have locks, she thought, *but what kind of lock can't be seen?* She turned the book over in her hands. *Some type of magical security added by a jinni*, she thought. She had originally found the book in Jacqueline's room, after all.

So how did Bloise unlock its secrets when I had made them all vanish? Maybe, she thought, *the spell wasn't meant to stop someone from reading the book altogether, but to deter me specifically from finding out certain things.*

Kiami lifted one hand toward her mouth and began chewing at her nails. Until Rhiannon's illness and death, Jacqueline had always been there for her.

She did her best to think only of herself and her guardians, then flipped the book open.

A hand-drawn illustration filled the page she had chosen. At the center was a door, surrounded by a smooth-looking frame. The space around the frame reminded her of the night sky, only not the one she was used to. The constellations and planets weren't right.

Kiami pondered what the piece of artwork had to do with her. The image itself held no writing beneath it, and the pages on either side of the drawing were blank.

She turned another page, and thoughts of the image were forgotten as her eyes landed on flowing cursive, which she knew to be her mother's handwriting.

They are people of the stars, ever watchful.
She is but one of seven unique children of this world.
Alive in the sun and shining silver at night.
We must keep her, our gift, safe from he who scatters darkness before him.

She flipped to the next page to find it filled with what seemed to be an account of her first growth spurt, several weeks after she had been in their care. Kiami concentrated her eyes on the words, not really reading them, and brought up a memory of how the mountain had looked as it crumbled.

The words began to fade.

6

Emily - Before All Else

The Human Realm

"Think about what led you forward to begin with." That was what the old wizard Bloise had said when they visited him.

Emily wondered if he had been referring to the wisps the whole time. They had, after all, been present since the start, intervening when they could, she supposed. If that were the case, remembering their time with him wouldn't do much good, not now that Blaine had shown himself to Kiami.

Emily gently chewed at her lower lip as she and Kiami flipped through the pages in Rhiannon's journal. After their earlier discussions, she had offered to share her mother's book to look for clues about the missing half-blood, but so far they had found no direct mention of any of them within its pages.

Although she dove right in, neither of them had been sure it would contain any answers. She had tried to remain hopeful, overall, but she could not seem to stop the low groan as it rose up from somewhere

31

inside her. Half the day had passed, and it felt to her like they were wasting their time scouring the book for nonexistent clues.

Kiami looked up at her from the pages. "Is it really that boring?"

"No." She shook her head as she said it, knowing the truth was that she somewhat doubted Kiami's idea it was the jinni that had spelled the book and not Bloise himself.

"It just seems like it takes a lot of concentration for you to keep the words on the page, if you stop reading."

"I know. But I am trying my best. I'm just not sure where to find the answers, and when I read some of these passages, I start trying to force connections, and my mind wanders, then the page fades..."

Emily placed a hand on Kiami's shoulder. "I wish we could know more about Amanda's visions. Maybe they would give us a clue."

Emily had been wishing that Amanda had told her details about what she saw when she was forced behind the eyes of a fellow half-blood. Amanda had tried, but so much had been going on at the time. Etzion had shown up hurt, accompanied by the imposter Aeron, and Emily had been struggling to understand her own abilities.

Emily removed her hand and stood up then stretched before turning her eyes back to Kiami.

Her friend slid a small, torn piece of paper into the book and then closed it gently. "Well, what did she tell you?"

Even though Emily knew Kiami had been in her owl form at the time, and given her enhanced hearing, probably knew exactly what Amanda had claimed, she replied, "Only that she had been having them since before she had taken Jacob's powers, to free her and Aden from his control. And that we had been in them, of course. How about you?"

"I mean, after you took off that day, she really didn't say much else on the subject."

"I know we can't, but I wish we could go and ask her." Emily sighed. She regretted not having been a more attentive listener. Looking back, it felt as though at that point they had already been through so much together. Now, she couldn't even remember why the reveal had made her upset to begin with.

Kiami stood, then pivoted to place the book down on the desktop. "I think we should take a break, anyway. Maybe we are looking too hard. I feel like the answer is already here, but we are missing it. I need to get out in the fresh air, clear my mind."

Emily mumbled, "Okay."

Kiami put a hand on her shoulder. "You still have our gemstones tucked away safely?"

"Yours, mine, Justin's, and Etzion's, anyway," she responded half-heartedly.

"When you say it's time to go, I think we should bring them."

Emily smiled up at her. "Go enjoy the outdoors, Kiami. Clear your head."

She knew Kiami loved to be out with nature; she craved it, but had Emily also noticed a twinkle of excitement as she left the room?

Perhaps, Emily thought, Kiami's spirits had risen even more, despite the fact that they had found nothing substantial in the book.

She had the feeling Kiami was still holding something back from her time on the mountain, but she assured herself that if it had to do with the task at hand, she would have spoken up.

Before she left them, Amanda had told her that she needed to take charge. To be a warrior. And if she could not trust her companions' decisions, what kind of warrior or leader would she be?

Emily made her way to her room but hesitated as she clutched the strap of her red backpack in one hand. She was reluctant to carry the powerful gems it contained away from the protection of the village.

On one hand, she agreed with Kiami that the group should keep the stones close. On the other, she had seen firsthand, now more than once, that they could be harmful as well as helpful.

7

Kiami - MIA

The Human Realm

Kiami had been fighting the urge to break away from her and Emily's research for what felt like hours, trying to ignore the desire to spend some time in her owl form. She was starting to feel drained from the effort, and the enthusiasm she had felt about conquering the fading passages seemed to dwindle into nonexistence.

Then, while they were chatting about the visions, her owl had sensed a difference in the atmosphere, and she gave in. She had a feeling things were going to change fast.

Once she made it out of the house, she underwent a quick transformation, then flew straight toward where the anomaly had occurred: Justin's house. Or at least what was left of it.

Justin's family home was a sorry sight. The fire that had started during their conflict with Aeron had done an enormous amount of damage, and given the fact that he had already lost his parents, she thought he was holding up well.

She wondered how much of anything could still be salvaged as she waited patiently outside for the cause of the atmospheric change to make an appearance.

When Etzion exited the front door, clutching a small instant picture in his hand, she was relieved. She remained in owl form, following out of sight as he made his way toward the house in the image, and realized that despite the fact that she hadn't had much of a chance to get to know him, she felt a kinship with him.

She wasn't sure if it was a byproduct of their shared heritage or the fact that he inadvertently reminded her of Fizzle in the way that he moved around using teleportation whenever it seemed to fancy him and not just when he needed to jump from realm to realm. He would be walking a straight line, see a mailbox or something else in his path, and he would simply blip past it.

She doubted Etzion even realized he did it most of the time. She figured it was second nature to him, the same way she would start to change into her owl form without really thinking about it or Emily would feel a pull toward someone that needed to be healed.

Watching this similar pattern of movement, she could not help but wonder where the little monster was. She missed Fizzle and wanted to make sure he was all right. The fuzzy monster popped in and out of her life so frequently, often just when she needed him, that she could not help but wonder if he had some sort of extrasensory perception when it came to her and her companions.

The teleporting critter had, after all, come to their aid at just the right moment on more than one occasion. He had even shown up in the Chaos realm and caused a distraction when a strange, tentacled plant had attacked them.

While he darted around the creature, they had managed to escape. She would have been worried that he had not, but later that day he had shown up again, after she had crossed the lakelet to explore, popping out of a pile of leaves and causing her a momentary fright.

The realm had been full of so many dangerous oddities that his startling reappearance had been a welcome sight. But the distressed cries of her friends from the other side of the water had propelled her back across to aid them. Then, after their quick departure from the realm to get away from the angered rock monster, she hadn't seen him again.

Even though their reunion had been short-lived, if she had a human mouth at this moment, she would have smiled at the memory of how he was often there one moment, gone the next. Sometimes he would reappear quickly, a few yards away, or on the other side of a wall, but occasionally he would vanish for a few days at a time, no doubt returning to whichever realm he came from.

She hoped Fizzle would make an appearance soon.

Kiami perched on the roof of a neighboring house as Etzion approached the porch of the home in the photo. He paused to wave at someone hidden from her line of sight. Then his hand closed and dropped back to his side before taking an awkward step away from the porch.

She cocked her head to the side, curious at his reaction, then heard Justin bellow, "Don't come any closer."

Kiami lifted her gray and silver wings, preparing to glide down and change back into her human form.

"It's just me, Etzion."

He lifted his hands in front of him and let the picture fall to the ground, showing his empty palms as Justin retorted, "I know who you are."

She leapt and maneuvered her owl body to land in front of Etzion, changing her form almost instantly as her talons hit the solid ground.

Etzion's eyes were wide as saucers. She quickly spun around to see Justin, his face tense, holding a flame-engulfed fist up at the visitor.

"Justin, this is no way to treat a guest."

His brow unwrinkled at the sight of her, and she blurted, taking a step toward him with each addition, "A friend and one of us."

When she was close enough to reach his arm, the flame went out, and she looked into his eyes. "He didn't cause any of this, not even what happened to your house. Not really."

"I know that, Kiami."

"And Emily will be relieved to see him. You know she is ready to move on. To look for the seventh."

"Precisely!" Etzion exclaimed, causing Justin's face to tighten back up as he stepped to the side and looked beyond her to address the newcomer.

8

Amanda - Pebbles

The Chaos Realm

Free to do as she pleased, Amanda made her way back to the garden path, then headed toward the pond. As she passed by the spot where she had met with Howin and Dhruv earlier in the day, a thought struck her: for all she knew, the pebbles could very well have been in the bag when she first received it.

Although she doubted Howin and Dhruv could have unknowingly passed the pebbles to her, even if the gloves in the bag had padded the bottom and stopped them from clinking together. The pair were very thorough in their duties, and there was a rule against using village property to carry personal items.

She concluded that they either knew the pebbles had been inside all along because they put them there or they hadn't been there when she received the tools.

Amanda clutched the bag tighter as she continued to make her way around the pond, meaning to get to the spot where she and the others had fled from the rock monster. She returned often, hoping to see the start of new growth in the area. So far it had remained unchanged from the day she arrived.

She tried not to dwell on it. Today she chose the location for a different reason. It was one of the safer, quiet places where she could inspect the pebbles without fear. Even during daylight most of the villagers didn't venture to the area for pleasure, and she understood that unless provoked, the creatures beneath the surface wouldn't bother her.

Once on the other side of the inlet, she sat down in the shriveled grass a few feet from the shore and spilled the colorful pebbles onto the ground in front of her.

She moved the seven small pebbles around, then lifted each one to better inspect them. There were no markings on them that she could see. The paint itself was flat and dull and in a single shade per rock, with only one exception.

She lifted the glossy pebble back up. When she did, a silvery blue translucent sheen from beneath the top layer shimmered as it caught in the rays of the sun overhead.

The reaction reminded her of Kiami's moonstone, causing a nervous tickle to erupt beneath her skin. Amanda shifted her weight and looked over her shoulder at the empty field beyond her as she questioned herself.

Perhaps, she thought, *I'm seeing something that's not there.*

She separated the pebble from the rest, then picked up the black one and moved it to the new pile. She did the same with the purple stone, then the green one.

What remained in the first heap were, yellow, orange, and blue. She selected the blue stone next, thinking of Etzion's gem, and added it into the larger group. Only two remained.

Amanda shifted her weight again as her unease grew. She doubted it could be a coincidence that so many of the stones represented the colors of the gems she and the other half-bloods had received. Someone knew who she was, and they were letting her know.

Unsure whether she should take the discovery as a reassurance or a warning, she concealed the stones within the inner pocket of her cloak, retrieved the tool bag, and headed back to the inner village.

9

Emily - Safe Travels

The Human Realm

Justin's voice rose through the open window outside. "You realize the girls have no idea where to start?"

Emily peered out, chewing at her lip as she wondered who he could be arguing with, but Justin and whoever he was talking to were out of sight.

"That's why I came back," a voice she didn't recognize retorted. "There was a rumor about a thing so strange, I thought maybe it was just what we were looking for."

It could only be one person. Relieved that he had returned before they left the village, she shouldered the bag and raced down the stairs to greet Etzion.

When she reached the porch, Kiami shrugged at her from between the two. The silver sheen in her eyes and the similarly colored streaks in her hair seemed to shimmer in the light of the sun and almost made her seem carefree, but the stiffness of her stance told a different story, as if she was ready to intervene at a second's notice.

Etzion looked up at her, drawing her attention away from Kiami, and acknowledged her with a nod as he continued to address Justin. "I went there and saw them for myself. I think they could be who we are supposed to be looking for."

She hadn't had a chance to talk to Etzion after he recovered from his time with Aeron. She could now see that like her own eyes, his were dotted with flecks of coloring. Although his were a bright blue, like sapphire instead of the purple amethyst coloring of her own. As if some of their gems were inside them.

Emily scrunched her nose up at the idea, remembering that Amanda carried a black diamond, and yet her eyes held a bright red hue.

Knowing that her own eyes hadn't changed until she found her powers, and Kiami's had always been as they were now, just as Kiami had always possessed her abilities, the coloring, she supposed, had to do more with their true natures coming forward than with the actual gemstones themselves.

Since he was facing away from her, Emily cleared her throat to let Justin know she was there so he wouldn't be surprised when she spoke.

He was clearly still on edge, despite the fact that when they had been chatting with Kiami on the porch after her return, he had insisted they were all safe. She waited a few seconds then said, "Hello, Etzion."

Etzion gave a half smile as he addressed her. "I found the picture you left me."

He motioned toward the Polaroid on the ground. "That was some smart thinking on your part. Giving me an image to look for after I returned to the house."

"I can't take all the credit. It was really someone else's suggestion." Emily smirked. "But thanks."

"Where's Amanda?"

She responded, "We need to go on without her for now."

Justin had seemed to relax little by little as she and Kiami filled Etzion in on all that had transpired since he returned to his family to recuperate. He even broke in to tell him about some of the strange things they had seen in the Chaos realm, such as the flowers that had eyes and seemed to bleed when they were hurt.

Once she was satisfied they had told him everything, including how they had bribed the old wizard Bloise for information, she asked him if he had any questions.

He shook his head before adding, "It sounds like a lot has happened to all of you. I'm just sorry it took me so long to return."

He wrung his hands as he continued, "And I hate to rush you, but I wasn't joking when I said we should hurry."

"I'm ready," Kiami offered.

Justin added, barely above a whisper, "As long as he's telling us everything."

"Amanda trusted him, and I do too," Kiami responded.

"That's good enough for me," Emily interjected. "Let's go."

"Do you still have my gem, Emily? I can transport us all."

She clutched the strap of the bag. "I do." Then, to remind him that each time they used them, the barriers that separated the realms seemed to become damaged, she added, "But remember, we should use them sparingly."

He nodded, then moved farther from the porch. "Come on, hurry. Who knows how long she will be there?"

Kiami appeared beside him. "Yes. Let's go."

Emily glanced over to Justin, and he nodded in her direction, then winked before speaking. "You heard the girls. I'm outvoted again. Let me grab our stuff and we can be off."

Emily smiled back at him, relieved that he sounded more like his old self. She knew that he just wanted to keep them safe, and as he passed by her to grab their other backpack, she silently promised to do her best to help him when he struggled with his anger before he could overreact.

When Justin returned with the rest of her supplies, she asked, "So how does this work?"

She pulled the sapphire from her pack and moved toward the waiting trio to hand it to him.

"It's fast." Etzion lifted his hand and snapped his fingers. "Like that."

Kiami tilted her head. "I think she meant, do we need to hold hands or something."

"Oh," he shook his head, "just stay still. I have to picture all of you there with me, as you are now."

Emily's skin tingled with what she could only describe as an electric charge from Etzion's magic. It seemed to spark along her arms, yet it didn't burn her or cause real discomfort. It reminded her of the spark from a lighter that refused to ignite.

Then, like a glitch, the sensation stopped, along with every other thing she felt and heard. For a moment, she was swallowed by a strange feeling of nothingness. It only lasted a millisecond, but in that instant, she felt as though she didn't exist at all...

Then she was back and once again felt her heartbeat, her feet on firm ground, and a breeze on her bare skin, and she sighed with relief, even as she wondered about the strange but brief hiccup.

We're all here, all together, she reminded herself as she opened her eyes and looked from person to person, pondering whether or not they had experienced the same lack of feeling. She shrugged it off and cleared her throat before asking, "Where are we?"

"That's debatable," Etzion said earnestly.

The bluntness of his statement gave her pause, and she breathed in deeply.

Wherever they were, the smell of caged animals hung in the air, and she tried to look past her travel companions. A thick haze filled the world around them, but it seemed to be clearing up by the second.

"What do you mean?" she questioned as she squinted at the blurry image of the large, colorful tents clustered around where they stood.

"Well, it's a traveling show. Sort of a festival of arts and the imagination. Only it's not where I left it. I think we are lucky we made it here at all..."

Remembering that he needed to have been someplace in order to teleport there, Emily asked, "If it moved, how did we find it?"

"Well, I told you I was afraid we would miss her, so instead of remembering the location, I concentrated on returning to the show itself. I knew that my sapphire enhanced my powers enough to take others with me, so I gave it a shot."

Emily glanced over to Justin and saw his face reddening. Knowing he would react to the news, she reached for his arm before he could make a move. "We made it. That's all that matters." She moved her hand down his arm and grasped his clenched fist. "And Etzion didn't mean to put us in danger, did you?"

"We could have all been lost in a void," Justin responded in frustration, then started to pull his hand away from hers, but at the sound of Etzion's voice, he hesitated.

"It's not like we were hopping from realm to realm," Etzion added as he threw his hands up and took a step back. "But I am sorry. I guess I didn't think it through."

A wheeze escaped Justin's throat, as if Etzion's words had caused him to deflate, and as his clenched fingers loosened, Emily worked hers into his until they were holding hands.

She thought of the silent promise she had made herself just before they left. She needed to keep him grounded, not just because it was what a good leader would do, but also because she wanted to. She cared what happened to him, despite the ways he had changed.

She gave his hand a reassuring squeeze, then looked from Etzion to Justin before locking her eyes on to his. "We will all make mistakes. We have to try to trust each other. It's the only way we can all get through this."

Justin returned the light squeeze. She smiled up at him and winked, knowing he would appreciate the gesture.

Music began to drift to her ears, and voices rose all around her, causing her to look away from Justin. The fog had almost cleared, but the more it dissipated, the louder everything around them became. As she tried to take it all in, she felt a sudden weight on her shoulders. It was too loud.

Some people called out in thundering voices for their friends to come closer in order to have a look as they squealed with delight while others barked orders in angry tones. Yet in the space that lay beyond her vision, all around, the music played on. At first, the sound had been giddy and upbeat. But as the remaining haze drifted away, the noise became a cacophony of instruments, as if all the musicians in the world were playing a different song at the same time.

It was true that she hadn't been given the opportunity to be around many crowded places. She thought of the bustling marketplace she had seen on her way to visit Bloise. There, the packed street was filled with stalls and people milling about. In that instance, she had wanted to stay to see more, but this was different. The crowd here was much larger, more rambunctious, and the noise was much more intimidating. To her, this seemed like a stuffed school auditorium with no chairs multiplied by a thousand.

She had never been to anything quite like it, but she seemed to be the only one in shock. And she again had to remind herself that she had in fact lived a pretty sheltered existence, at least after her eleventh birthday, when she had been imprisoned in her home much of the time.

She couldn't help but wonder if Kiami, with her heightened senses, experienced all the world in this way. Emily allowed her eyes to drift over to her and found that despite the fact that Kiami had remained silent since they had arrived, she was smiling in her direction.

Perhaps, Emily thought, *since Kiami has always had these heightened senses, and she can use the sound of her own voice as a weapon, she enjoys the noise.*

10

Amanda - Unintentional Harm

The Chaos Realm

Given no choice but to cease her inquiries about Bly, in a last-ditch effort, Amanda entered the dining hall, took a random selection of soup and a piece of fruit from the buffet-style line, skipping over the other options, then sat near the entrance. Her stomach was in knots as she stirred the contents of the bowl with her spoon. She doubted Bly would show up. Not after he had caught wind of the thing she had accused him of, although she took solace in the idea that if confronted, he could prove his innocence by producing his tools. If he had in fact put the stones in the bag, he would want to keep his distance from her.

Amanda let her spoon sink to the bottom of the bowl and left it there. There was no way she could eat.

She had started her search for Bly with her eyes but had ended up talking to more people than she had the entire time since she had arrived in the Chaos realm. No one seemed to know of Bly, or if they did they didn't dare to tell her. She hadn't realized her mistake until she had said too much.

Thinking she was being cunning in her approach, she began to tell a tale about how the volunteer she had worked with early in the day had accidentally left one of his own loaner tools behind.

She had known that misuse of the loaned property was frowned upon, but she had never before witnessed a punishment for the indiscretion. Her sheer naivety at the impact it could have on Bly was lost when her questioning piqued the interest of one of the wall guards.

She soon realized she was drawing undue attention to herself, and the innocent Bly, when the guard stared hard at her with his single eye, as he cited time in the stocks at the forest's edge as punishment.

Remembering her own experiences there, Amanda paled at the very thought of it, but she had already said too much. As he expertly turned her questioning back at her, she relented, excused herself, and apologized while she insisted that she must have had the name wrong.

Disgusted with herself, Amanda left her bowl where it was. There was nothing else she could do tonight, but she promised herself she would tread more carefully when it came time to speak with Howin and Dhruv.

11

Kiami - Welcome to the Show

The Human Realm

Kiami thought Etzion wasn't wrong in his description. The traveling show was in fact a montage of the imagination or a festival that was a collective of souls dreaming out loud in song, music, dance, and activity. The colorful tents encircled and enclosed the space they entered, brightening the dull brown dirt beneath their feet. The largest one towered above the others and seemed to melt into the clouds at its highest point.

The aroma of cooking meats and candied treats hung in the air, sweet and sickening at the same time. A man on stilts tottered as he moved among the crowd, waving and smiling from ear to ear beneath the powder and paint that covered his face.

A little farther away, a woman dressed in a shimmering blue costume waved a paper fan below her nose as if she were fighting heat rather than trying to conceal her youthful, blushing cheeks from the muscular man in the tightfitting singlet that appeared to be holding what looked like a heavy metal safe above her head for the crowd's pleasure.

Close by the pair, a man with a painted face twisted skinny balloons into odd shapes and handed them out to younger members of the ever-growing audience, while beside him a young girl with a breast pocket full of art brushes held her pallet high as she offered to decorate the crowd's flesh with images of animals, plants, or any other oddity they wished.

The place was alight with the magic of human storytelling and art, yet for all the mirth around her, she sensed something else as well: an undercurrent of suffering, hidden below the surface. There was something hard, something dark, lurking here.

She could feel it, but even as the goose bumps rose on her arms, she continued to smile at Emily, because at that moment to her the young woman seemed like a butterfly just escaping its cocoon. The notion reassured her that Emily would be able to help them through this until the end.

Emily couldn't feel it, the darkness, at least not the way she could, but she was open to understanding how they each felt and why, even more so now that she had finally come to terms with the fact that Justin would never be exactly how he was before, and that none of them would be, for that matter.

The growth was apparent to Kiami by her actions as she watched Emily give Justin the reassurances that he needed in order to deescalate the situation, once it had come to light upon their arrival that Etzion may have put them all in danger because of his rush to get here.

Deep down, she knew Justin couldn't help but be protective. He had always felt a bit out of place among the people in the jinn village, believing himself a singular oddity.

None of them really knew Etzion as well as each other, but he had fought his own battles while they were enduring their trials and tribulations, and she expected that Justin would warm up to him once he had a chance to get to know him better.

Emily motioned for her to move forward, and as she went into the crowd, the feeling that something was not right here grew.

The performers began to maneuver their routines toward one of the tents, and the majority of the crowd followed, moving in a way that reminded Kiami of how people were drawn to follow her when she sang, as if they were compelled to keep up. But these people participated in this dance of their own free will.

It wasn't long before they had all been ushered inside the largest of the tents. Rows of chairs encircled all but the opening she had entered through, and as Etzion sat, Kiami was quick to follow. She was curious to see where this was going.

In the lower center of the tent, at about eye level, a net that had been attached to four towering pillars was stretched out several feet above the ground. The sturdy-looking pillars themselves rose high above, each ending in a lower-case T-shape just below the tent's roof. A single empty swing hung down well below the arms of each T.

In the upper centermost part of the tent, a large metal circle dangled at about the same level as the swings, suspended there as if attached at the tent's peak of the fabric by thin cables that even someone with her exceptional vision could not make out.

As she looked on, one of the swings started swaying rhythmically back and forth, as if a rider had started to pump its legs. She moved her eyes back over the others, but they remained still. Kiami returned her gaze to the moving swing and watched on in silent anticipation, even as the crowd around her erupted in cheers and a booming voice sounded from in front of her.

"Ladies and gentlemen, today you will embark on a journey of mystery, magic, and wonder..."

The commotion escalated as the crowd clapped in response, and the announcer, no longer willing to compete with the ruckus, paused his speech.

After the furor died down once more, he continued, "Please, allow me to introduce our cast." The people around Kiami again clapped enthusiastically, and in that instant, out of nowhere, a figure appeared on the swing.

It was the blushing woman Kiami had seen earlier with the strongman. She still wore a shimmering outfit; the sequins on this one were bright red, no doubt to help the audience focus on her from where she swung above their heads. This more form-fitting ensemble came complete with matching gloves and a flashy feathered headdress.

As the woman began to wave down to the crowd in their seats, Kiami looked around, baffled, wondering where the woman had come from and how she could have missed her entrance, or how the woman could have hidden herself from her vision.

Kiami lowered her eyes to examine the rest of the crew that were lined up for the introduction. To her disappointment, she saw that while she was distracted by the swing, several large, brightly colored cages had been wheeled into the tent, housing exotic-looking animals. Each cage was labeled in scrawling print to designate the occupants. A man with a whip stood close to one of them, which read only *The Beast*.

The catlike creature inside didn't look much like a beast to Kiami. In fact, the way the spotted feline pushed itself against the corner of the cage as it cowered made her think that the handler was the beast in the scenario. Disgusted by the scene, she resolved to find a way to help the captive animals, before returning her focus to the cast.

She recognized the man with the stilts from outside; another with similar face paint balanced on a unicycle beside him. Several people juggled various objects, and a woman held a torch in front of her face, puffed up her cheeks, and then blew so hard, the fire reached out toward the crowd.

There were three fellows in the lineup who wore outfits of shimmering red sequins, similar to the one the woman on the swing wore. Although athletic-looking, the men appeared to be much older than the woman in the air. Graying hair hung just below the napes of their necks, and unlike their female counterpart, the men's faces were weathered by age.

Kiami was jolted by a sudden clashing boom as the sound of a hammer on a gong rang out. The attention-grabbing noise was followed in quick succession by a new proclamation from the announcer,

"Without further ado, welcome to the show!"

His latest exclamation was met by a fresh wave of cheers. For the first time, Kiami looked at the announcer. He grinned from ear to ear from beneath his top hat as he waited for the most recent disruption to die down, and as it did, he waved one finger, showing off his velvety-looking black-and yellow-suit, and added, "Quiet, please."

As the lights dimmed, a hush fell over the crowd. Then the familiar thud of a spotlight seemed to echo throughout the tent.

"Newly returned from retirement, the aerobatic stylings of Jasmine!"

A low murmur ran through the crowd, and Kiami watched the beam as it appeared then lifted upward and onto the occupied swing. The woman was now upside down with her legs holding her to the seat as her arms hefted forward. Still perplexed by the woman's initial appearance,

Kiami squinted and stared hard.

Something dangled from around the woman's neck. It appeared to be a piece of jewelry that twinkled each time the spotlight hit it. The reaction reminded her of her own moonstone, and she clutched at the base of her neck where it had once hung as she wondered if this woman could be the one they were looking for.

"Kiami."

She pulled her eyes away from the woman and to Emily.

"Etzion said she's not here."

Taken aback, Kiami dropped her hand. "She's not?"

Emily shook her head, then whispered into her ear, "Let's go outside so we can hear each other."

She cast her gaze back up at the swings. The rest of the troupe had made it to the woman's level, occupying two of the previously empty swings. One swung alone from one corner while the other two swung together, one dangling from the other person's hands like a human chain.

"Kiami," Emily said again in a hushed tone, "come on."

Reluctantly, she stood up and followed the others.

Outside, the music played on while a mixture of folks milled about. Some of the people looked downright scruffy and unkempt, yet others wore suits and dresses while they walked around arm in arm. From their drastically contrasting appearances, Kiami assumed they were both crew members and visitors who were now taking advantage of the less crowded walkway as they chatted about various wares and services sold during the show. Kiami had barely noticed the vendors on her way in. Some of them seemed to have stacked cardboard boxes to use as makeshift tables to display their offerings, and Kiami guessed that most of them hadn't even been set up when she initially walked through.

A sudden jerk on Kiami's arm pulled her between two of the tents. The space here was deserted.

"Are you okay, Kiami?" Emily asked, concerned.

Kiami visibly shook, as if trying to shake herself back into focus. "Yes. I guess I just got caught up in the show."

"Geez. It had barely begun," Justin teased.

Kiami shrugged. "What now?"

"We can check the other tents," Etzion said reassuringly. "She's got to be here somewhere."

"Does she?" Justin blurted, mocking their companion. The corner of one side of his mouth lifted in a half smile as he added, "Is there anything you aren't telling us?" He lifted his eyebrows. "You didn't seem very surprised that she wasn't in attendance at the show."

"Well," Etzion looked down and shuffled his feet as he replied, "she may not have seemed very happy about performing when I saw her."

He took a deep breath, then looked back up and added, "I don't think she was a willing participant. She caused some trouble when they brought her into the tent."

"How so?" Emily asked in a steady voice.

"You saw the strongman, the one that lifted the safe above his head?" Kiami nodded in unison with the others.

"She lifted him up over her own head and tossed him like a rag doll."

He paused as if thinking and then added, "I don't think she's dangerous to us. No one wants to be caged."

Kiami's cheeks burned, but it was Emily that spoke out.

"Caged?" Shock had lit up her features. "Caged!" Emily repeated and shook her head, then turned to the closest tent and began trotting toward it.

Kiami followed close behind her, detecting her frustration and outrage at the situation. She had been captured herself once, but it had been short-lived, and Amanda hadn't really been trying to harm her, whereas Emily had been kept locked in her room like a monster for a long time by a family that really wished she had not been there at all. She knew Emily could certainly empathize with the girl, but she wasn't quite sure how she would respond to it once she saw it first-hand.

As Emily reached for the closed flap on the tent, Kiami reached out and made a light grab at her arm. "Wait a second."

Emily looked up into her eyes, pleading with her to let her go. "We need to find her."

"I know. But let's just not go rushing into tents, blindly."

Justin interrupted, "Should we split up?"

"No," Emily said without breaking eye contact. "I don't think we should. There are only a half a dozen tents beside the huge one the show is in."

Kiami flashed her a one-sided smile and removed her hand.

Emily turned to Etzion and asked, "Who or what are we even looking for?"

"Her name is Tarah. She's ... well, you will know her when you see her, I am sure of it."

12

Amanda - Unrest

The Chaos Realm

Amanda's anxiety worsened as the night went on. She tried to sleep but found it impossible to do so. After a tumultuous few hours of vivid disaster-fueled thoughts, she gave up on the idea altogether.

She sat up, wishing she had requested a larger personal space so that she could expel some of her nervous energy. As it was, she had accepted the smallest room available, containing just a bed, a sitting desk, and a closet.

It wasn't safe to venture outside the village walls at night, and in her current state Amanda didn't think it was wise to wander inside them either. Like many places, even the nicest neighborhoods still harbored seedier elements that became more apparent as the light disappeared from the sky. The village here was no exception. While many people lay in their beds asleep during the darkest times, the inner streets here became a different place during those twilight hours.

Instead of trading time and skills for a safe place to sleep and food, inhabitants took to the streets to trade in magic. Some were looking for the benign, but there were also those that sought spells and potions for more malevolent purposes.

Stalls at the trading post area that held fruits, spices, clothing, and other everyday items morphed as they were restocked with potent herbs, hexed candles, and enchanted artifacts.

She thought of the market they had seen on their way to visit Bloise and wondered if it changed in a similar way after dark. Emily had seemed especially interested in the wares there, and Amanda was sure that if they were here now, both she and Kiami would have enjoyed inspecting what the merchants here had to offer, even if doing so would earn them sideways glances in the morning.

Amanda smiled as she thought of some of the less eventful times they had shared. Brief periods when they had been able to relax and joke with one another. In truth, there weren't many. It seemed something was always waiting around the corner for them to trip over, but the few good times they had were worth thinking of, even if her friends could never forgive her for the things she had done.

The thoughts and memories of her friends had soothed her nerves just enough to allow sleep to take over. Now Amanda woke up with a start, afraid she had overslept.

Even though it meant she had only dozed a short time, relief washed over her as she made her way to the window and saw that the first rays of illumination had barely begun to light up the new day.

She threw her cloak on, then slung the tool bag over her shoulder, but as she reached for the rake, she hesitated.

Instead, she turned to the closet to retrieve her staff. Most mornings, she left it behind, hidden under some second-hand clothing she had acquired during her stay.

At first glance, as she uncovered it, the staff was almost unrecognizable. Her gem, which was enclosed by the thin branches at the top, was covered in a thick layer of clay-like mud, which she had gently applied when she first sought refuge here. She had figured the ruse would dissuade potential thieves and help hide her true magical nature.

She stared at it for several minutes before she thought better of it. Her gem often got her into as much trouble as it got her out of, and she had to bring the rake. Carrying both would only slow her down.

With the decision made, she threw the clothes back over it, swung the door shut, and grabbed the rake before heading out of the village.

Once beyond the walls, Amanda hurried toward Howin and Dhruv's meeting place. As she sped past the entrance to the circle garden, she threw a fleeting glance in its direction. She would have to skip the ritual this morning. She wanted to be the first person there when the pair took up their post.

Clearly not expecting anyone to show up at this hour, she found them still sitting atop the seat of their small, covered wagon. At the sight of her, they hopped down almost in unison, causing the bull-like creature that was hooked to the front to look up from the portable wooden trough as it placidly chewed its breakfast.

The animal glanced from its masters to Amanda with its fly-like eyes, and she couldn't help wondering if it saw a hundred small versions of her in its lenses. She peeked down at its food but was quick to look back up at the animal and away from the mixture of bloody red meat and leafy greens the trough contained.

Still focused on her, the animal snorted in her direction and then lowered its head back down to continue consuming its messy breakfast.

Amanda looked away from the animal and found that Howin and Dhruv had made no move to reach their post, a few feet away. Instead, the pair were staring at her in much the same way she imagined she had been staring at their bovine: a look of silent astonishment.

Perhaps, she thought, *they didn't appreciate me interrupting this animal's meal.*

She shifted on her feet and cleared her throat. "I'm sorry. I wanted to, um, ask you guys something. I mean tell you guys…"

She shifted again, thinking of the painful scarred tissue she had seen on some of the arms of other volunteers. "There was something in my tool bag yesterday that I don't think belonged there…"

She handed her rake forward, and Dhruv, who was closer to her, accepted it so she could remove the tool bag from her shoulder. "I took them out…" She tested the words and looked back and forth between the pair, but neither creature so much as blinked.

"I knew they shouldn't be there."

Dhruv set the rake at his bare, clawed feet and reached for the bag, rifled through it, nodded at his partner, then set it beside the rake.

As his eyes locked on to Amanda's, his ears stiffened, and he crossed his arms over his chest, making it known that he was unimpressed by her attempt to get answers.

Howin still looked relaxed as he took a few steps to get closer, then pointed at her shoulder. Knowing he was waiting for her to return the brooch from the day before, Amanda reached to unclasp the beetle as she tried to explain. "I just wanted to make sure something hadn't changed, and maybe I didn't understand my job…"

Howin let out an annoyed hiss as he shoved a hand into one of his pockets and brought out a pencil-shaped twig and a small book for recording notes. He scrawled something onto it before tearing the page out. His eyes slitted as he shifted on his feet, then folded the page in half and jutted it out at her.

As she handed the brooch forward, swapping it for the folded page, she noted that Howin's fur had puffed out around his neck, and his ears now looked just as rigid as Dhruv's.

She opened the page and glanced down at the simple sentence: *Tools are where they need to be.*

Amanda felt her brow furrow, but she bit her tongue as she refolded the note and placed it within her cloak's compartment. Her throat felt dry, and she swallowed to try to calm the feeling. She was floundering, she knew it by the changes in the pair's demeanor. Even if they had something to do with the pebble's placement, they wanted nothing more to do with her questions.

When she looked up again, Howin still held the returned brooch in one fist while he reached into another pocket with his free hand.

Amanda backed up a step. She had never seen an exchange happen like this before, and the pair seemed to be more agitated with her by the second. Her first instinct was to continue retreating, and she had to focus all her attention to remain in place when his hand reemerged.

He held a tree-shaped brooch, which he shoved toward her as if he was anxious to be rid of it. Amanda reached forward to accept it, but as she looked down at the symbol, she hesitated with her fingers hovering just inches from the piece of metal. It was the one she had been waiting for all along, the one that would give her entrance to the stone-faced carvings.

Howin pushed the pin toward her again, then let out another hiss, drawing her back from her sudden stupor.

"Sorry." Amanda apologized once more, then snatched it up and affixed it to her sleeve. With the brooch in place, Howin passed her a small parcel tied closed with a piece of twine.

Just as she accepted the package, the bovine let out a sharp, bleating sound, drawing her attention back to it as it lifted its head just above the now empty trough, then its midsection lurched forward as a yacking sound emanated from its throat over and over, until the food landed back where it had started. Amanda couldn't help but glance down at the contents. They were now covered in mucus and appeared to be half melted together.

Her own stomach hefted at the sight, and she covered her mouth with her hand, but nothing came up.

When it settled a bit, she glanced at the pair again, wondering if she should make another attempt at her inquiry, but when she made eye contact with Howin, he made a shooing motion, and she realized the pair were waiting for their bovine to finish its meal before they moved to their post.

Glad she hadn't had an appetite the night before, she turned away from the animal and made her way to the garden chore she had been assigned. She hadn't accomplished what she had come for this morning, but she had managed to get what she had needed all along.

Amanda knew what she was expected to do with the parcel, but she also realized she may never get another chance to be here, at least not with permission. Her heart raced as she neared the first carving and lowered herself down in front of it. Dried leaves crackled as she raked them away from beneath the face with her hand.

She was supposed to choose one of the three and place the parcel within the upturned palm of the stone hand. The action would then activate the fountain, and water would trickle from the carved eyes, down the protruding cheeks, imitating tears.

To her, the face on the wall looked just as crudely carved as those on the topiary, with the exception of the eyes themselves. Lashes had been added at the top, as well as deeper lines showing the top and bottom of the lid. Even the pupils at the centers seemed better carved as they held even shallower indentations for additional texture. Small ears were added to each side, within the square about halfway down, and no nose had been created.

Amanda repeated the inspection at the second carving; the only notable difference was the shape of the mouth below the eyes on the nose-less face. The first statue's mouth had been no more than a thin line, as if it was supposed to appear to be drawn closed. This one's mouth was open, but its eyes had been chiseled with the lashes at the bottom, as if they were closed.

The third carving's eyes and mouth were open, but it didn't just lack a nose; the ears themselves had never been added.

Amanda sat back on her heels, thinking. There were only slight variations to the facial features, and the protruding hands on each looked almost identical. The instructions for the chore were very specific, and Amanda repeated them in her head as she had learned them from the archives in the library.

Whispering to herself as if trying to convince someone else nearby, she said, "There has to be a reason they only leave one offering at a time."

She removed the tied parcel from her pocket and placed it into the palm of the carving. The hand made a slight shift with the weight of the parcel, then the tears appeared to well up from beneath the carved eyelids. It looked like magic, but sense told her the weight of the parcel caused the flow.

Still curious over the fact that she was only supposed to activate one fountain, she couldn't help but wonder what would happen if she were able to get all three going at once.

Amanda reached into her pocket and felt the smooth stones hidden there. Testing their weight in her hand, she pulled them out. The parcel had not weighed very much, and in theory she surmised that a couple of the stones would do the trick just as easily.

She moved to the next fountain and placed three stones atop the hand. It shifted, just as the last one had, and the statue began to cry in the same way.

Amanda moved to the last statue and repeated the action with three of the stones, but the hand failed to shift into position. She let out a frustrated groan, then made her way back to the second carving, but it only took her a moment to realize her mistake. The stones were not identical in size and weight. She returned to the unactivated fountain and dropped the remaining stone into the hand.

A smile erupted on her face as the palm shifted and the eyes welled up.

Perhaps, Amanda thought, *the colored stones wee given to me for a reason after all.* Knowing she might never find out exactly who gave them to her, she whispered a triumphant thank-you to no one in particular. The only fact she knew for sure was that whoever it had been went out of their way to paint the stones in particular colors that she couldn't disregard.

Within moments, shrill whirring sounds grew all around her as if somewhere close by a dormant machine had clicked on. She backed up from the fountain, as far as she could without getting caught in the short trees, then turned in a circle, trying to pinpoint where it was coming from. But a small tremor reverberated under her feet, sending her back to the wall she had just moved away from.

This wasn't the first time the ground had shifted below Amanda's feet, and she stared back at the space, expecting to see a collapsed section where she had stood.

Instead, a metal hatch about the size of a manhole cover had been unearthed. Amanda took a step toward it and then squatted down to touch the cover with her hand but pulled back as her fingertips came into contact with the hot metal.

Then the hatch that had been triggered by the fountains began to slide open.

13

Kiami - The Wrong Idea

The Human Realm

The first tent they peeked in had housed a sort of mess hall. Folding metal picnic tables ran parallel to one portion of the edge. The rest of the outer rim was home to a few crates, each of which appeared to be filled to the brim with a variety of pots and dishes. These sat on the ground below several camping stoves that were set up for use on top of well-worn sawhorses.

The next two tents were crowded with sleeping cots in various states of disarray. Both, Kiami thought, smelled like a footlocker, but the second one's scent had been so putrid that she continued to pinch her nose closed for several seconds after she left the enclosure.

The fourth tent housed a small stage and some temporary bleachers, which they ducked behind in order to avoid being spotted by the two muffled voices arguing, which drew near only moments after they entered.

"Why are we hiding?" Etzion asked in a low voice.

"Are we supposed to be in here?" Emily whispered back.

"Probably not, but I didn't see any signs saying it's off limits," he offered with a shrug.

"If they really have a person caged up in one of these tents, do you honestly believe they would welcome us snooping around?"

Etzion shook his head.

"Do you think they will come in?" Justin whispered so low, Kiami could barely hear him.

Emily put a finger to her lips in response, then dropped her arm and tried to squat lower.

Kiami inched to the edge of their temporary hideout and peeked around the side. Someone was holding the tent flap open. She whipped her head back quickly and nodded at her companions to indicate that they were in fact coming into the tent.

A woman's voice rang out. "You boys were ready to put me out to pasture, can you imagine! My own sons!"

Kiami peeked back around the edge as she heard the shuffling of their feet moving closer to the stage.

The woman had her face turned away from Kiami, but there was no mistaking the red sequined outfits the pair had on. They were from the aerobatics routine.

They must have finished their portion of the show, Kiami thought.

"And after all that I have done for you. I made sure you had a good childhood," the woman proclaimed as she tossed one of her sequined gloves onto the stage and quickly began removing the other from her fingers on the opposite hand as she continued to address the troupe member that accompanied her. "So what if you had to move around? I did my best. The shame of it." She dropped the second glove down, then turned her face to look at the man, giving Kiami a better view.

"You boys are lucky that I found a way to bring our troupe back to life after you let it die."

The woman, Jasmine, if the name of the troupe was any real indication, wrinkled her nose at him, then smiled. "That worthless magician! Can't even make someone disappear properly. I should take his job too, don't you agree?"

The man remained silent.

Jasmine's smile morphed into a sneer. Kiami heard her click her tongue as she wrapped her hand around the jewel at her neck, then repeated the question, "Don't you agree, son?"

The man gave a slow, controlled nod before he spoke. "Yes, Mother."

She responded excitedly, "You're darn right!"

Mother? Kiami wondered at the sight of the pair as she inched her way back.

Jasmine looked very young compared to the man she called her son. Her hair showed no visible graying, and from here her skin looked taut and smooth. Surely that couldn't be her child. If anything, Kiami imagined, the situation would be reversed.

Jasmine's voice took on a serious tone as she continued, "Now, grab that crate from behind the stage. We have to get back before the finale."

"Yes, Mother."

14

Emily - The Show Must Go On

The Human Realm

Emily lifted her eyebrows at Kiami as her face emerged from the side of the bleachers. She hadn't been able to see the duo that had entered the tent, and she was curious about their conversation that had been taking place near what she assumed was a practice stage.

Once the rustling of their feet died away, she asked, "What was that all about?"

Kiami said, "I'm not sure."

Emily righted herself, then moved to dust off her clothes.

"There was something strange about them," Kiami added thoughtfully. "Etzion, are you sure Tarah is the person we need to see?"

He nodded.

"Let's check the next tent then. Only two more to go," Justin offered.

The fifth tent was set a bit farther back from the rest, but just enough that it didn't break the circular shape they formed. Unlike the other tents they had visited, this one had wooden signage hanging outside the closed fabric flap. It held the same sprawling lettering the cages in the show had held. This one read: *Tarah the Terrible - No admittance.* Below that, a piece of cardboard had been taped up, and someone had written in what appeared to be powdery white chalk: *Attraction closed for maintenance.*

"Tarah the Terrible?" Justin questioned. "This is who we are trying to find?"

Emily threw him an annoyed look and shushed him before opening the flap and stepping inside.

Cages of metal and wood, in various shapes and sizes, littered the ground in what appeared to be a haphazard arrangement. Some were occupied and others appeared to be empty. Dusty carpets and a few partially filled water dishes lay on the ground for the handful of uncaged animals that were instead tethered to stakes by short lengths of rope. Most of the animals seemed to take no notice of her as she entered, and even the ones that did look up curiously made no noise, even after her companions followed behind her, and soon lost all interest in their arrival.

Emily could only imagine how Kiami felt about the situation. She was, after all, sensitive about the mistreatment of animals. She looked over at her friend and mouthed, "Later."

She felt a familiar pull toward the centermost point, where the largest of the wooden cages sat facing away from them. This one had wheels under it, like the ones that had been brought into the main tent for the show. Although she couldn't see the occupant, she didn't care. Whoever was inside was hurt.

As she moved toward it, Etzion whispered, "Emily, wait."

She paused and turned around.

"That's hers," he said, pointing to the wooden cage, then he began nervously wringing his hands in front of himself as he spoke again. "Remember, despite her appearance, she's just a girl. Er, young woman, that is."

She responded with a silent thumbs-up, then turned away, rolling her eyes. She understood better than he knew. Just because Tarah was caged didn't mean she was a monster.

Realization dawned on her, and she turned back to face him. He didn't know her story.

"I do understand. Trust me."

He threw her an appreciative smile, and she returned it before spinning back around to make her way to the cage. The pull was getting stronger, and as Emily turned the corner to face the bars, the familiar static sound filled her ears.

The kneeling figure in front of her lifted her head to look up but remained where she was. Her powder-blue complexion looked unearthly against the red hair that spiraled down from her head, landing on the dirty blanket wrapped around her shoulders.

Emily took another step forward and then paused as their eyes met.

She waited as Tarah lifted a hand from beneath the covering and grasped one of the metal bars with it.

"You don't work here," she sneered at Emily, revealing the tips of her sharp teeth. Her voice hardened. "Couldn't stand not getting to see a glimpse of Tara the Terrible, huh? Well, you've had your look. Get out."

"You're hurt," Emily answered as she held her hand out and moved closer. But as she prepared to release her healing magic and reached to touch Tarah, the girl shot to her feet and backed away, dropping the blanket in the process.

"Don't touch me."

She heard Justin exclaim, "Wow."

Then she heard Kiami's voice. "Tarah, don't be scared."

But the static sound was beginning to drown out everything around her, and she could scarcely focus her eyes on the person in front of her.

Emily tried to keep her voice steady and soft. "Please. Let me help you." She had already initiated the use of her magic, and it screamed from within her to be released.

She closed her eyes and pushed her hand between the bars. As soon as she felt Tarah's flesh against her own, in retaliation, she let the wave of her magic wash over her, relieving her of the push.

As the static died down around her, she opened her eyes and went down onto her knees. She knew the reprieve would only be temporary. Eventually, she would have to release whatever it was that she took in when she healed people, or it would fester inside her like an unattended wound.

Justin kneeled in front of her and lifted her chin with his finger to look into her eyes. "When Tarah reached for your arm with her four hands, I thought she was going to tear it off."

"What?" Emily assumed she had misunderstood, but as she pulled her chin away and moved her eyes around him, she realized she had heard him clearly.

Tarah was looking herself over, while all four of her arms moved as she did. When she finished her self-examination, she let the appendages fall at her sides, one set below the other.

When her eyes met Emily's, she spoke. "How did you heal my cuts?"

Although Emily could no longer tell where the blood had initially come from, she noted small, congealing pools of it around the area where Tarah had been kneeling, as well as a trail that led to the back of the cage where she had stood.

"It's just what she does," Justin responded nonchalantly, then questioned, "What realm did you come from?'

"Realm?" She scoffed, breaking eye contact with Emily. "Now you sound like Bavmordia."

Emily could hardly believe her ears. "You met Bav?"

Tarah nodded before answering, "She's the sorceress that did this to me. I was just a normal high school student. I changed after she gave me this."

She lifted her hand to show a dark blue rune embedded on the flesh of her palm. "She called it my lesson."

Emily remembered how she had thought the sorceress looked like a timid librarian when they had met, but the ruse had been short-lived, and she had managed to escape. Curious about how Bav had ensnared Tarah, she listened intently with her companions as Tarah told her how she had come to be inflicted with Bav's curse.

"I don't know how long she had been watching me, but I have had a lot of time to think about everything since it happened. The large leather boots she wore threw me off a bit, but when she came to my door, I thought she was just a salesperson. She was so insistent, and once she had me under her opal's spell, I couldn't say no. She wore it around her neck, and every time I tried to ask her to leave, she would touch it.

"After she grabbed my hand, I remember trying to wash the rune off, then I started to transform into this, and Bavmordia said I was going to be the monster I behave like," she explained.

"She wasn't wrong, you know. I was a bully; I was mean and greedy. I was just what she was looking for. She told me how she had always been drawn to humans but that a long time ago the realms had been created to keep magical beings like herself from having access to humans."

"Did she say how she got through?" Kiami interrupted.

"She didn't explain exactly, only that she was delighted to find herself here. Although, I think I might have an idea how.

"I didn't really believe her, you know. The story she told, even as I was becoming this. She looked at me almost apologetically as I panicked and pleaded with her to take it back. Bav said she couldn't, that she had made sure of it. She said it would go away on its own after I learned my lesson and promised to keep me safe until then."

She gulped. "I knew that if my parents saw me, she wouldn't be able to, though, and I was right."

A tear trickled down one of her cheeks as she continued. "She did try. I was the one that froze up when the men came to take me away.

"It all happened so fast. By the time I started to fight back, it was already too late. I remember it had just begun to storm, and the air outside felt heavy with electricity. Bav was shielding herself from view with her magic, but when lightning struck, I caught sight of her form and broke free.

"I managed to reach her, just barely, as another bolt lit up the area.

But as I struggled to grasp her, I realized something else had too. Something much stronger than me. I could make out tentacle-shaped appendages flailing above us, reaching through a hazy area just beyond her.

"One wrapped itself around her and started to pull her away. As it did, in my attempt to hang on, I grabbed her necklace, yanking it free. In the next lightning strike, I saw her face again, but it wasn't the same. She looked as if in those seconds she had aged hundreds of years."

Tarah closed her eyes for a moment, releasing a haggard breath as she did, then added, "One smaller bolt of lightning shot down as I was being dragged away, but she and the creature that had occupied the space were gone."

Justin sat back and sighed. "So Bav got dragged into another realm?"

Emily threw him a look and then said, "Not now. Tarah, how did you end up here?"

"The opal," she said matter-of-factly. "After some time, I figured out how to use it to make me invisible, and I escaped the asylum my parents sent me to, with its help. But I had nowhere safe to go. With how I looked, I figured a place like this would welcome me, and I wasn't wrong."

"But they aren't treating you any better than they are treating these poor animals," Kiami said.

"No." She sighed again. "They treated me like a star. But I did something stupid."

A sudden ruckus erupted outside, and Etzion spoke up. "The show must be over. We need to let her out before someone shows up."

"You need a key," Tarah said.

"Where is it?"

A clapping noise erupted behind them, and Emily spun on her heels.

"I can answer that," a familiar voice responded.

15

Kiami - Not So Surprise Party

The Human Realm

With what she had seen earlier, Kiami wasn't the least bit surprised by Jasmine's interruption.

"You gave the gem to *her*," Kiami announced, pointing at the aerobatic athlete. Once she had heard about Bav's rapid aging when her opal was removed, she thought of Jasmine, her vanishing act, and the strange conversation she had been having with her too-old son, and it had all fallen into place.

"This one's quick," Jasmine replied, pointing at her own head. "Did she tell you why? She wanted to redeem herself. She thought helping out an old woman would make her curse go away. And when it did not, she wanted the opal back."

"No. I want the opal because you can't handle what it's done for you. Being young again wasn't enough for you."

"I want more. What is wrong with that?"

"She can keep the opal, we don't care," Justin announced.

"Yes, we do, it's obvious she can't handle the responsibility," Tarah urged.

Jasmine lifted her arms. "I'm right here."

"See what I mean?" Tarah responded. "Never enough attention."

Justin retorted, "Listen, lady, you have no idea what you're dealing with."

Emily crossed her arms in front of her chest. "Give it a rest, Jasmine. Kiami, Etzion?"

Without a word, Kiami changed into her owl form and began to move toward the woman.

The woman's face contorted in surprise, but as she turned to flee, Etzion appeared behind her, grabbing her shoulders.

Justin approached the woman as he spoke. "Nice work, you two, a little flashier than was needed but whatever."

Kiami watched as he reached out and removed the necklace, which he carried over to Emily.

The woman changed quickly, and Etzion released her shoulders as the wrinkles embedded themselves in her face, showing her true age. She slumped forward, then lowered herself to a sitting position.

"I only wanted what I deserved."

"And we are only returning you to your natural state. Before the opal came into your possession," Emily said. "You can't control and hurt people to get what you want."

"I was a good person, and where did it get me?"

"Your sons were only trying to get you into a comfortable home. They wanted to take care of you, as you had them when they were young. They weren't trying to throw you away."

"I know," she croaked. "But then you offered me another option."

"You should go talk to your sons. See if they can forgive you for using the opal on them," Tarah offered.

She started to push herself back up to her feet, and Kiami saw Justin and Etzion rush to her side to help her up.

"Thanks." She huffed, then reached into a pocket and pulled out a key, tossing it at her feet.

"Begone, Tarah. Whatever this really is, I want no part of it." Then she turned and made her way out of the tent.

Justin let out a heavy breath. "Is it me, or did that go a little too easily?"

Kiami couldn't help but agree, but unable to speak in her current form, she bobbed her head up and down. Right now, she was a little anxious at the idea of transforming back so soon, and her intuition said she should stay alert.

She made her way toward the prison, still in owl form, as Emily unlocked it.

"What now?" Tarah asked as she stepped out of the cage.

Justin pushed his dark hair back. "She's not one of us."

Emily scowled. "If she wants our help, we aren't just going to leave Tarah unprotected. You heard her story. It might mean she's not who we came here looking for, but we could still take her with us."

He raised his eyebrows. "To the village?"

Emily put her hands on her hips as she continued. "Why not? She would be better protected there."

"What if something more dangerous comes looking for her?" he argued. "The village isn't impenetrable. You pointed that out yourself, Emily."

"Yeah, well, it sounds like Bav moved into then back out of the human realm through weakened barriers. It may not have been us that caused both of the disruptions, but you can't deny that at the very least our use of the gemstones could have helped create the second one, the one that sent Bav back, and away from protecting Tarah. Meaning she's another casualty, interlocked with us through no fault of her own."

"But I was at fault. I mistreated everyone around me," Tarah interjected. "Then I went and gave the opal away."

Kiami thought Emily must have heard true sincerity in her voice, because she reached up to place a comforting hand on her shoulder. When she did, the pair seemed to lock eyes, then Tarah spoke again. "I really did think helping someone else could end the curse, but it made everything worse..."

As if she was hoping to alleviate her guilt, Kiami watched and listened as Emily removed her hand and interrupted her confession. "Do you know what I think, Tarah? I believe you haven't forgiven yourself yet, and that's why you're stuck like this."

Kiami let out a screech of approval, then Tarah bent down and looked into her owl eyes. "Neat trick."

"That's Kiami, and I'm Emily, by the way. And this," she said, thrusting the opal talisman out in front of her, "should stay with you. Whatever you decide."

Justin kicked at the dirt as he asked, "Is your name really Tarah?"

She nodded, and Etzion jutted his hand out for her to shake. "Nice to meet you up close. That's Justin, and my name is Etzion."

Satisfied that the others were capable of continuing their introductions without her, Kiami unfurled her gray and silver wings as she made her way toward the edge of the tent, letting out a low screech. She wanted to spend more time in owl form before she changed back, and scouting the area would help put her mind at ease.

As Kiami readied herself for flight, the air outside seemed lighter, and she wondered if Jasmine had caused some of the darkness she felt just by having Bavmordia's talisman in her possession.

Music still played from somewhere nearby, but it was a softer, sweeter, and more controlled sound than the earlier melodies. To Kiami, it seemed like the show was done for the day. A few people wandered about between the tents, but the only chatter she could hear came from inside them. Regardless of appearances, she circled the encampment twice, looking for signs of an angry mob or anything else out of the ordinary that could have been caused by their use of Justin's sapphire.

Satisfied, she headed back toward her friends as sunset blossomed on the horizon, looking as if a million small fires had ignited all at once. It was a soothing sight, but it meant that darkness would be coming quick, like the closing of a velvet stage curtain, and she was the only one in her group that could see well in the dark.

As she neared Tarah and her friends, movement near the only tent they hadn't visited caught her eye. This tent was set back slightly from the others, not enough to break the circle but enough to create a larger space between it and the rest, which she supposed would offer slightly more privacy.

Kiami shifted her wings to glide in closer for a better look. She landed as softly as she could on top of the tent, then made her way to the edge. As she peered over, she saw several young men standing at attention, like toy soldiers. Then the young men became a single young man.

Kiami tilted her head to the side. The young man became a group of twenty, then back to one, then two, then one again. The action reminded her of the shuffling and spreading out of a deck of playing cards.

There didn't appear to be anything behind him that would cause such an illusion or manipulate his appearance in such a way.

She backed up and moved to the farthest edge from where the young man stood, then jumped off to glide down to the ground.

Kiami was cautious as she made her way around the side of the tent. She didn't want to spook the young man by drawing attention to herself before she got close enough to get a good look at him, but as she neared the area she estimated he had been in, she discovered that he was nowhere in sight.

With the intention of doing a more thorough search, Kiami returned to human form, a decision she regretted immediately.

Kiami whispered, "Is anyone there?"

She listened hard to the sounds around her, then she spun in a circle to survey the area. Hoping no one had witnessed her change and annoyed with herself at her carelessness, she returned to the tent where her companions waited to tell them what she had seen.

16

Amanda - Rabbit Hole

The Chaos Realm

The subtle vibrations beneath the trees had caused many of the flower petals to detach from their branches. Amanda was reminded of slow-falling snowflakes as she watched them cascade down, creating a colorful blanket over the grass.

A sharp click sounded as the hatch opened its full width and the whirring gear noise came to an abrupt stop.

Amanda inched toward the hole and leaned forward to peer over the edge. Below the access portal, half-circle steps protruded out from the right side and descended into the darkness.

They looked to be made of metal, like the rounded top that had slid open. Amanda reached in and felt the step with her fingers, then her palm. The step lacked the warmth she had felt radiating from the cover.

Amanda sat back on her heels and concentrated. Her heart thrummed from a mixture of excitement and worry. She listened harder, noting that the trickling of the fountains had ceased as well, and she wondered if somewhere a countdown had begun. With no idea how long the opening would remain in place, she knew a decision had to be made.

Inaction would lead to nothing. She hadn't come this far to find herself too scared to continue. As she stood, her robe got caught underfoot. Worried that it could happen on the stairs, causing her to stumble, Amanda removed her outer garment and left it in a heap next to the opening.

She stepped down onto the first half-moon-shaped stair, then wrapped her arms around her midsection. The skin on her natural arm felt clammy to the touch, and her heart began to pound harder, echoing in her ears.

Trying to calm herself, she closed her eyes and took three deep, controlled breaths. With each intake and release, she willed her heart rate to slow.

She dropped her arms back to her sides and took the next step, eager to find out what awaited her beneath the garden.

The air below the surface didn't seem stale, and Amanda wondered how it was being ventilated, although she supposed it was of little consequence in the grand scheme of things. As it was, the farther she descended, the harder it became to see the next step. The stairway seemed to be lit solely by the light that made its way in through the open hatch above her, so she made slow, measured movements forward.

As Amanda reached the bottom step, she hesitated. She could see a floor spreading out for several feet in front of her, but beyond that there was only darkness.

She scolded herself for her reluctance. This was not a simple game of hide-and-seek. She was standing in the middle of a war between a powerful father and his cunning daughters, and she had lost a lot in the crossfire. Friends, her father, her mother ... other innocent people had been caught in it as well.

She needed a resolution. She needed it to end. She urged her feet to continue their trek, even as the hair on her neck prickled and her throat contracted in a low groan. She wiped at her damp cheeks. She had been concentrating so hard on her movements that she hadn't even realized she had been crying silent tears.

She cleared her throat as she stepped with one foot, then the other. With her full weight bearing down on the floor, a rectangular panel became illuminated beneath her, lighting up several meters of space around her.

Amanda pushed on. The farther she advanced, the farther ahead the floor lit up, exposing the empty white walls of a vast corridor.

When the door first appeared in the distant haze ahead, Amanda thought her eyes were playing tricks on her as they adjusted to the ebb and flow of the fluorescent-like lights. But the closer she got, the more the image in front of her solidified, and she found herself face to face with a smooth metal doorway.

There was a single palm-sized button on either side of the otherwise empty frame, which was lighted from behind, illuminating carved runes. One glowed red and the other green.

If this had been a human device, Amanda would have automatically made an assumption about which meant "open." But this was something else. She did not recognize the runes, but someone had added the drawn-on image of a bird of prey to the green button.

The crude bird outline reminded her of Kiami, so without much more thought, Amanda pressed it. As she lifted her hand back up, the door began to slide sideways, exposing the entrance. She stepped across the threshold before she could second-guess her actions, and the room lit up just as the floor of the corridor had.

Amanda felt a crop of goose bumps rise on her arm, and she tried to rub them away. In the human realm, places like this underground hold would not be unheard of, but Amanda had never seen something quite like it in any of the realms where magic was prevalent.

It seemed to her that science and advancements in technology had gone in different directions, and although magic and science coexisted on some level in each place she had been, science played a smaller role in all but the human realm. Something she didn't think was so strange.

It just seemed appropriate to her that nonmagical beings would have more of a need to create solutions with technology that magical folks could otherwise handle with simple spells or their ingrown abilities.

It wasn't a large space. A stiff-looking padded chair was bolted to the ground by a single solid metal leg in the center of the room, and Amanda walked toward it, then reached out to feel the leathery brown fabric that covered it.

The armrests at each side looked as though they could be flipped open to reveal something stored within, but when she tested the idea, she found that neither would budge.

She looked up and turned around the room. The wall that the door was centered on appeared to be painted black, apart from the door frame itself. In stark contrast, the walls on either side of her were white, like the corridor had been, but were covered in identical square panels outlined in light gray. Yet the opposite wall between them looked more like a large movie theater screen than a solid wall at all.

Amanda approached it and placed a hand against the thick fabric. It gave in slightly beneath the pressure, and as she pulled her hand away, the indentation it made remained for several seconds before filling back in.

Her shoulders slumped as she let out a deep sigh. She had been expecting more. Frustrated, she made her way back to the chair and sat down hard.

A low, consistent beeping noise sounded from the doorway, and she looked up as the opening began to close. She bolted up from the seat and raced to the door just as it finished sliding shut.

With this side lacking the runed buttons found on the corridor side, Amanda tried to push the door with all her weight, but it refused to budge. She was trapped.

In a frenzy, she clenched her fists as she backed up, meaning to run at the door.

But as she reached the side of the chair, she stopped, and her breath caught in her throat. The solid dark wall around the door had changed.

It was still black as pitch in the background, but it now held a pattern of twinkling lights. The colors ranged from light yellows to pale blues, even vivid reds and purples. Some of them were spread out, covering the whole of the wall, while others seemed clustered in various shapes and sizes, from tiny specks to fist-sized plates that glowed.

Amanda reached forward and touched a large red sphere with her index finger. It bobbed backward, then swung forward into place. As it did, the wall rippled outward like water, causing each light it touched to shift up and then back down with the movement, as if they were floating on liquid.

She reached forward again, this time aiming for the blackness. But when her finger made contact, it didn't have the same effect, and the wall felt solid beneath it.

Amanda lowered her arm, then moved to the next wall. This section still looked the same, but she held her hand out and ran her fingers against it for the entire length, just to be sure.

Now, instead of anger, she felt confused. This was far different than anything she had seen in any of the realms. She almost wished for a monster to appear; at least then she would know how to react.

With the thought, a hum of static filled her ears, but it wasn't her shadow magic calling to her from within. It was different. The low sound was coming from the wall that she had thought looked like a screen.

Amanda moved back to the chair and sat, spinning the seat toward the wall. The fabric now looked pixilated and fuzzy. She squinted her eyes and stared, barely blinking. As an image began to come into focus, she relaxed and sat back. Something was happening.

Three shrouded figures appeared on the screen, and as they did, she heard the words, "It's you," coming from the space in front of her, as if speakers were concealed somewhere nearby.

"We have been waiting a long time for you, Amanda."

"And who, exactly, are you?"

"We are the sisters you seek. Sophia, Akila, and Mia," said the centermost form.

Amanda rolled her eyes. "How do I know that's true? You can't expect me to just believe it. You are only an image on a screen."

"For our own safety," one of the voices answered.

Amanda folded her arms over her chest and then added, "I need proof."

The figure in the center turned her covered head to the right side and nodded, then repeated the action on her left.

The pair wasted no time transforming, but instead of the owl form Amanda had become accustomed to Kiami using, they changed into something closer to what she would consider taloned hawks. One was covered in steely gray feathers and the other had a rich brown along its wings, while its underbelly was a much paler shade.

Amanda's face tightened as she looked skeptically at the birds of prey. She thought the remaining figure must have noticed the change, because she spoke up.

"Kiami can become an owl, yes. But we can become any bird of prey we wish. I, for one, have always had a fondness for vultures."

Amanda, thinking she had misheard the figure, repeated, "Vultures?"

"Yes. Like the ones you drew during your imprisonment below the Arcane castle."

She uncrossed her arms and sat up straighter. "Fine. What is this place?"

"A watch post of the stars. Like Hara Berezaiti."

"The mountain?"

The figure gave a quick nod then added, "You would have found a similar room had you chosen to explore the steps that went up ... but you could not have spoken to us there. Our father has disabled the communications systems in most of these places, and that's why we needed to lead you here."

Thinking of the mountain, Amanda had to wonder if they weren't somehow below her, although she hadn't seen any other obvious openings inside the room or in the corridor.

"Where are you?"

"We are close enough. But no, we aren't exactly in the realm with you."

Amanda didn't bother masking the irritation that crept into her voice. "I thought you were trapped. Unable to help stop the celestial."

"Yes. Our father had trapped us. But although the people in the Chaos realm fear him, they don't want to be under his control any more than we or you do. Some of them have become very good at doing what he commands while diverting his attention to help in our endeavors."

Amanda sat forward. "So, you're saying you're free and you're doing nothing."

"We are waiting, thinking." The shrouded figure paused, then lifted her arm and twirled her finger in the air. "We know what you think you want. But there are many things to ponder before we can help."

"To ponder whether the barriers should stay or go? Haven't you had enough time to ponder?" Amanda snapped in frustration.

The figure moved her head from side to side, then answered, sounding a bit vexed herself, "To decide if we should take back control, and we decided that it's not up to us."

Amanda could hear her heart in her ears as she responded, "If not you, then who?"

"Why, you," she answered in a calmer voice, raising her hand again as she did, this time holding her palm up and open. "Now, hear me out before you say more."

Amanda looked down at her lap and then pushed herself back in the seat. When she looked up again, the figure continued, "We have had a long time to think, Amanda, and we aren't sorry we disobeyed him, the celestial, our father. But who's to say who is truly right and who is truly wrong? We choose you because despite the things that you have endured and the power we gave you and helped you nurture, we might add, you try to hold on to that last shred of empathy and hope with all you have. It's a rare thing. Even our own Kiami, an optimist at heart, struggles from time to time, and you are the one that has sustained the brunt of the damage inflicted by our father."

"Any decent being would try. But I have failed, more than once."

"Less than you know, dear. And you still try, even after what you consider to be failures or flaws in yourself. In fact, your friends are about to see first-hand how greedy some people can be when given the opportunity. It's kind of a pity you will not be there to witness it."

Amanda pushed herself forward in the seat again. "Are they in trouble?"

"Nothing they can't handle. Worry not."

"Is someone going to die?"

"Who cares? What's one more life in the grander picture?"

Amanda paled as she thought of how she had been willing to give up after the loss of her arm. The way she had been pulled by someone or something out of her nightmare and into the dream realm where, while her arm regrew, her thoughts of giving in to death were replaced by anger at the realization that she had no choice but to go on.

"I care! If it's up to me, then I don't want any of you to have control. Not him, and not you three. To me, you all seem the same. Maybe we should be allowed to make our own mistakes, decisions untainted by a so-called higher power. If we fight each other and ruin the planet, it's our own fault. But we should be allowed the chance to learn and grow unencumbered by any of you."

"Now we have come full circle, haven't we? You place the blame on us for people you lost, but haven't you done the same thing? Some of those things you consider flaws in yourself, taking lives when you see fit or when you felt pushed to? How are you any different then?"

"You force us to do what you want. You have me trapped in here now, so I can't just leave, and before, when I was ready to give up at the mountain, you didn't let me. Maybe I had a choice, but I was manipulated until I didn't feel like I did. I don't want anyone else to get hurt."

"They will. Either way. You can't stop that."

Amanda hissed, "You know what the real difference between us is? It's not that I won't do bad for what I deem to be the greater good. It's the fact that I know many of the things I do are wrong. Your father and you three, on the other hand, don't seem to."

She wanted to go on. She was filled with disgust at the way they were willing to put others in the line of fire but not themselves. She clenched her jaw, trying to stop herself from saying too much. In the end, she knew she needed their help to understand.

The figure snapped back, "You know nothing."

"I know the so-called *celestial* is flesh and blood, as I am sure you are too." Amanda hopped up from the chair in a rage. "Tell them to change back, then come out from wherever you are and talk to me in person!"

The shrouded figure didn't disappear from the screen but instead pushed her hood back, revealing raven hair pulled tightly against her head and then twisted into a bun at the top.

The woman's eyes held the same otherworldly coloring that Amanda had noticed when she met the celestial face to face, although on the screen the kaleidoscope that surrounded her irises didn't seem to be constantly shifting.

Her skin was not as fair as her father's, yet it shimmered in the same way his had, as if her cheeks and forehead were covered in a fine powder made of stardust.

"You are right. Akila and Mia aren't changing back to their human forms, because once they do they will need to find a source to recharge their energy, much as Kiami does. Where we are, we do not have access. None of us are immortal. We are flesh and blood, as you are. But our life spans are infinite compared to yours."

Amanda's eyes widened, but she wasn't satisfied. She raised her hand and rolled her wrist, motioning her to continue.

The figure's expression shifted as her eyebrows lifted to what Amanda thought looked like amusement before she spoke again. "We will have a hard time letting you go, giving you what you want. You have become much more in our and his fight to persuade you than we ever thought was possible. A true anomaly, but you don't understand how complex the situation is. Sit back down, and we can explain. Science as it is has developed here enough in the human realm that I think you will be able to follow."

Amanda reluctantly returned to her seat and crossed her arms.

"Imagine the human realm, only a whole planet of mundane individuals. Comparable to the humans here at about the age of three hundred thousand, scientifically. Now fast-forward a few thousand years. They strived to learn, to conquer life and death, to give the mundane abilities that made them naturally stronger, and to create a planet to replace their own should it be needed. The more they remedied, the more troubles they created. They found the only solution was to put laws into place stopping the use of certain technologies and ending practices that they deemed inhumane, such as creating new planets and using scientifically developed genes to create new races of people.

She stopped and looked up at Amanda. "Do you follow?"

"I believe so."

"Good. Now think of the myth the jinn told but imagine instead a couple who escaped their own galaxy, which had become filled with rules that they didn't want to accept or adhere to. These two believed they had transcended to a greater calling and decided they would go far enough away to be undetected."

"Your father's race started like the humans here?"

She shrugged. "Maybe he truly isn't human anymore. Perhaps none of us are, where he came from, yes. They were very much like the humans you know at one point, but they have been calling themselves celestials for ages, having advanced so much from their meager beginnings."

Amanda looked away, picking at her nails. She had considered the idea that the celestials really weren't from this planet, but to hear it all laid out was worse than she imagined.

"Well, what is to be done?" came an impatient voice from around the screen.

Amanda dropped her hands and looked up. "Is there a way to stop him or not?"

"If you truly want to be rid of us. But are you sure everyone will be happy with that choice?"

Overall, Amanda had learned that the people in the Chaos realm didn't want war; the Arcane may be another story, but she thought perhaps if they were free, that would change with time.

"I don't care."

"I think you do. Have you considered the problem with the barriers? The realms could hold for a millennia more if undisturbed, or they could crash down at any moment." She threw Amanda a knowing look and then began to pace back and forth. "One has a lot to consider when making choices that involve multiple forms of beings, millions of souls. Not everyone will be happy, no matter what decision is made..."

Amanda gawked, thinking she was trying to get her to change her mind.

"And what of the creatures in realms you have never ventured to, like the descendants of the beings of light and energy? How would they adapt if the realms came down after so long?

Many of them care not about the physical things in the world you know. They are happy with the realm they live in, unlike humans, the jinn, the arcane, and those in the Chaos realm. What about their choice? Not to mention we wouldn't be there to intervene if someone that became unhappy with your choices tried to take control after we left."

Amanda hesitated before she replied, not because the woman had caused her to reconsider, but because she wondered if she could really see it all through to the end. Amanda clenched her fists. Whether she was alone or aided by the other half-bloods, she would do all she could to rid the planet Sumir of the celestials.

"Yes, there are hard things to think about, and you must forget who you think you are supposed to be," the goddesses said in unison.

"Will you stop being dramatic and just tell me what we need to do?"

"There is a way we can take him and return him to his planet of origin, but we wouldn't be allowed to come back, and the people here, the planet would be left to their own devices for good, as you want. But it will be difficult for us to subdue him.

"Right now, we hover orbiting outside the planet, we are in a standoff. Our father knows that if he follows us, we will go straight back and take control before he can reenter the planet's atmosphere. But if we go now while he is aware, he will recapture us and the whole thing starts again.

"If you and your fellow half-bloods could distract him, make him drop his guard, and expel too much energy, we could force him onboard and into imprisonment, long enough to get him back where he originated from.

"We warn you; our father will not easily be fazed; it will take all of you, and he will be wary of the power you yield when you are together."

As the woman paused, Amanda asked, "How do we get his attention in the first place?"

"The gems you were all gifted were meant to be together, powering the barriers for the world for a millennium. Part of the pull you feel toward the others is the gems trying to reunite.

"The farther they are from each other, the weaker they become, and when you use one to strengthen yourselves and your abilities, it drains them or redistributes the energy away from its intended purpose. But when they are all together, they give off a unique energy frequency that will bring him to you."

Amanda gulped. She knew Emily, Kiami, and Justin had probably set out to find the missing half-bloods already. She wrung her hands, wondering how far they could have gotten and if Etzion could have returned to join them. "So the seven half-bloods all need to be together, but not until we are ready?"

"We will only have one shot at capturing him."

"How will we know he is drained of most of his power?"

"You will know. When he has been pushed to the edge, he will become something akin to a large cloud of dust and gas."

"He used my powers against me inside the mountain..."

The woman cut her off. "He redirected your power in the mountain," she corrected. "And he will seem even more unstoppable in this other form, but you must resist giving up. You and the others must push him to change, then hold him back until he has returned from the form. Only then will we strike."

And if we fail to get him to use all his energy, they won't intervene at all, Amanda thought. *They will abandon us.*

"Is this still what you want, Amanda?"

"Yes."

"Then you must go. The celestial visits the gardens here like clockwork at the start of the new moon. He likes to keep up appearances to keep the villagers in line. Our guess is you have less than a day to leave this realm and avoid his suspicions."

"How do I know you're going to show up in time or at all?"

"Trust me." Her mouth morphed into a toothy grin. "We wouldn't miss it for the world."

17

Emily - Indecisive Actions

The Human Realm

Despite the fact or perhaps because her own encounter with Bav had ended in a much more mundane way, Emily felt guilty for the fate that had befallen Tarah.

When Jasmine had appeared, she recognized the opal dangling from the woman's neck right away, and in her haste to correct the situation, she couldn't help but wonder if she had overreacted during the encounter.

Since Kiami had gone out to verify that the perimeter was uncompromised and appeared safe, she had been trying to distract herself from the notion by focusing her attention on the animals in the tent.

At first she had intended to release them all, but both Justin and Etzion had been quick to object, stating that most of the animals would have a tough time on their own in the wild.

Emily thought she must have been looking distraught at the revelation, because Tarah had come to her side and spoken up. "If it helps to know, the crew took good care of them before Jasmine locked me in here and kept them away."

"Is that so?" Emily asked.

Tarah nodded.

Emily released a loud breath then said, "Okay, well, would you mind helping me take a look at each of them before we leave, just to make sure they are all right?"

"Sure, but that might take a lot of time."

"Not if we help," Etzion suggested, pointing to himself and then Justin.

"I don't believe we need to rush," Emily added, thinking there could be other reasons why Kiami was delaying her transformation.

In an attempt to pass the time as they checked over the animals and filled their water dishes, Emily asked, "So, have you made a decision on whether you would like to come with us or not? I know you said that they treated you well before Jasmine."

"Well, they did. They kind of put me on a pedestal. But I'm not sure that's what I need. I mean, what happens if I change back?"

"When," Emily corrected her.

"The fact is, when I return to myself, they won't have a need for me here, and where would I go? I can't go back home. You probably wouldn't understand, but my own parents didn't even try to help me; they hid me away the moment I no longer fit into their idea of a perfect world."

Emily gave her a half smile. "Trust me, I understand, and it sounds to me like you have already made up your mind."

She was happy with Tarah's choice, and Emily knew that as long as she intended them no harm, Tarah would be able to enter the jinn village without a problem. Once there, she thought the young woman could start fresh, as she herself had.

Just as she was toying with the thought of telling Tarah about her own experiences with her parents, Kiami burst through the tent flap and looked around wildly.

"We have to leave. It's going to be dark soon, and we should head out beyond the tents where we arrived. The clearing around them spreads out for quite a way before it meets the edge of a forest on one side. I think we should make our way toward that forest before we use Etzion's gem."

Justin, who had been sitting on the ground with a ferret in his lap, jumped to his feet. "What's the sudden rush?"

"I saw something, someone like Aeron."

Etzion asked, "Did he attack you?"

Justin balled his fists. "Where is he now?"

"No. He didn't know I was there. I was watching in my owl form, but when I tried to sneak closer, I lost sight of him."

Etzion belted out, "Well, you don't have to tell me twice. Let's go."

Justin shrugged, then nodded.

Emily looked at each of her travel companions and chewed at her bottom lip as she thought for a moment. They all seemed pretty eager to leave, so she gave in. "All right."

She turned to Tarah. "Still want to come with us?"

Her newest companion tilted her head up and down in what Emily decided was an uncertain nod.

The five of them had exited the tent and moved down the dusty road in quick succession.

As they neared the outskirts, Tarah whispered, "What does that mean?"

Emily responded with a questioning look, unsure of what she was referring to.

"Kiami said he was like Aeron. What does that mean?"

Emily didn't pause in her forward movement as she responded, "Well, Aeron wanted to harm us. He tried to use Etzion to trick us into thinking he was one of us. It's kind of a long story."

Tarah stopped short. "Maybe I should stay here."

Embarrassed that she hadn't asked Kiami more questions to begin with, Emily barely acknowledged her response. Rather than rebutting her statement outright, she threw an apologetic glance over her shoulder as she hurried to catch up with Kiami, who was waiting with Etzion and Justin farther ahead.

"Where did you see him, the young man?" she asked as soon as she thought she was within earshot.

Kiami furrowed her brow as she turned her gaze to her. "He was near the last tent, the one we didn't go in."

"How exactly was he like Aeron?"

"He could replicate things, only instead of wolves he did it to himself," she explained.

"Wait, a boy that multiplies himself?" Etzion reached up and scratched at his chin as he asked.

Kiami nodded. "Like Aeron's wolves, they seemed to be copies of himself."

"What if he's..." Emily started, but Etzion cut her off.

"He could be the one we are looking for," Etzion said apologetically.

Emily turned her face to him. "What do you mean? We came here on your hunch to find Tarah."

"I'm sorry," he offered. His cheeks began to turn pink as he shuffled on his feet. "I just remembered something. Aeron had talked about a being that replicated himself, but after what happened, I thought maybe he was making it up. I mean, you guys never mentioned him, and I had brought it up to Amanda before I went home."

"Do you think Tarah knew he was here?" Justin asked.

Emily looked over her shoulder at the cursed girl. She seemed to be content to hang back for the time being.

Etzion spoke up. "Why, Justin? Do you think he is with the traveling show? I'm pretty sure I would have noticed that."

Emily shot them both a sharp look as she exclaimed, "That's enough. We are working together, remember?"

She turned toward where Tarah stood and motioned her forward. "Did you know there was someone here with abilities like ours?"

She shook her head fiercely.

She turned back to Kiami. "How are we going to find him now? The same way we did Tarah?"

"We can't search the tents in the dark and when they are full of people."

"Well," Emily offered, "maybe we should camp here? We have some supplies, and we could start a small fire."

"You think that would attract others?" Justin asked.

As Tarah bridged the gap between them, she said, "I doubt they would notice. Unless we are on top of them."

"Let's at least get farther from the show. See the tree line I was talking about, out there in the distance?" Kiami pointed. "Let's set up over there."

"It's settled then, we rest for a few hours. But," Emily suggested, "be ready to start searching at first light."

It wasn't until the last word made its journey from her lips that Emily realized how tired she was, and she covered her mouth as a yawn threatened to escape.

18

Amanda - Many Safe Returns

The Chaos Realm

Amanda made her way up to the garden top in a stupor. How was she supposed to go back and tell them what the children of the celestial had told her?

The sound of whirring gears activated as she passed through the opening, and Amanda watched in silence as the cover slid back across the gap.

When the noisy gears stopped, she snatched up her discarded robe and put it back on, then walked forward with her eyes fixed on the wall. Staring in an almost trancelike fashion, she moved them over the carving.

Even though the daughters of the celestial had promised to leave after his capture, she was still angry. An urge to destroy the fountains bubbled within her, and she wished she had her staff with her. If she, she would have made sure no one ever witnessed tears from stone again. Just like everything else, the carvings had been part of the plan all along.

Another manipulative tactic.

Amanda felt her shadow magic push and swell at her from somewhere inside, but she relented. Using her inherited magic could probably get the job done, but it would also set the celestial on alert when he discovered they had been destroyed.

She took a deep breath as she reminded herself that soon she would be reunited with the others and they could help her from here on out. The decision about the barriers did not need to rest solely on her shoulders. She could only hope that the other half-bloods would agree with what she had done, even if she herself had doubts.

She had felt justified in her decision to make the celestials agree to leave, but in doing so she had put herself and the other six like her in direct danger, a thing she had been trying to avoid by keeping herself in the limelight. She went to her knees as fresh tears welled.

Raising an arm to wipe her face against the coarse sleeve, she sucked in her breath as the weight of the brooch reminded her that time was short. The sun was waning, which meant she had spent the better part of the day below the surface.

With the celestial's visit eminent, she needed to clean up and tie off some loose ends before her morning departure if she hoped to conceal what had happened here.

If she weren't careful, the plan would fail before they even had a chance. If she hoped to avoid suspicion altogether, she needed to aim to erase her presence as much as she could.

She inspected the garden as a whole. Although the fountain no longer ran wet with tears, the gifts were still in place. She collected the stones from one, then the other, and dropped them down into the pocket of her robe.

It appeared that the trio was right; no one had entered the garden after her. The leaves and petals that were normally raked up and moved were scattered all about the garden, and she used her feet to sweep them off to the left and the right of the trail alternately as she made her way down it. She didn't have the tools or the time to do the job properly, but she assumed that the assignment had been given out and could only guess that someone was waiting to finish the task.

Once she was back on the main path, she turned to the circle garden. It was late in the day, but she wanted to visit one last time and feared that if she put it off until first light, she would run the risk of getting caught up in her own thoughts. She often did while she was there, and she couldn't chance an encounter with the celestial if she didn't depart early enough.

Amanda took her time walking around the topiaries. The silver feather was gone from the head of the tallest figure, but all seven of them now had newly embedded flowers at their bases. The tiny delicate petals appeared to be an identical species of plant, but the assortment of colors they displayed were so similar to the pebbles she had received that she stuffed her hand into her pocket and drew them out.

Amanda couldn't help but think it wasn't a coincidence. The gardens, although always well-kept, rarely had such changes imposed on them in the time she had spent here.

Amanda knew she could be overthinking it, but she couldn't help considering the idea that the person who had gifted her the pebbles might have added them in as some sort of message.

If it was a message, Amanda wasn't sure what it meant, but she thought maybe she would understand with time. She followed her previous route and inspected the figures again. As she did, she hid one of the stones below the foliage of each as a sign that she had seen the additions.

Amanda woke before the sun. She had endured another night of restless sleep, but she was eager to set about her tasks. She eyed the pile of lighter shirts and pants in the closet. Although nothing special to look at, they had become a much better option than her usual attire to wear beneath her cloak, since she had been volunteering for work, but she was glad that she didn't have a use for them in the human realm.

She retrieved her staff from its resting place beneath them, then donned her cloak and waited for the first rays of light to pierce the early-morning fog that had invaded the land.

Her first stop was the quarter keeper's office to quell any suspicions that could circulate over an abandoned room, but to her dismay, she found it empty. She had only met the keeper, Kaelah, once.

She was the only winged resident Amanda had encountered during her time here, and when they spoke Amanda had fantasized about asking her if she could fly with them, but she bit her tongue. As she waited she thought of those small, iridescent wings and how their shape reminded her of the wings of a dragonfly, but after a short time, she abandoned the task to make her way down the path to return her brooch.

As the sun rose higher, the fog seemed to worsen, and she squinted to see. She had no choice but to take her time or risk tripping and getting her robe caught on the bushes that lined the way.

She released a relieved sigh when she caught a hazy glimpse of the cart ahead. It wasn't until she was upon it that she noticed two figures standing where the pair she sought usually lurked, but both beings' stature was all wrong.

Amanda hesitated, scanning the area again, but Howin and Dhruv were not in sight. She had never seen them absent from their post by this hour, and she balked as she realized it was the quarter keeper who had taken up the spot in their stead. The second figure was handed a brooch and a shovel then spun and moved past her with quick steps.

She tightened her grip on her staff as she was reminded of how Bly had been nowhere to be found when she sought him out and now Howin and Dhruv seemed to be gone as well.

It was too late to turn back.

Kaelah had already seen her approaching and lifted a hand to beckon her forward.

Amanda forced a smile on her face. She hoped she hadn't caused the trio any harm, but she had no real reason to blame the quarter keeper for their absence, so she loosened her grip and advanced.

Below her long, slender nose, Kaelah moved the corners of her own mouth upward to mimic Amanda's when she approached.

As she removed the brooch from her sleeve and handed it to the quarter keeper, she blurted, "I was looking for you earlier. I see why I couldn't find you."

"Ah, are you leaving us?"

Amanda nodded. "I won't be returning anytime soon, I don't think. Feel free to allow my room to pass on and if you could, distribute anything useful that remains within to those in need as they were distributed to me."

Kaelah's wings fluttered behind her as she spoke. "As you wish." Then she leaned down and whispered, "Amana, please, on your journey home, steer clear of the inlet."

Amanda lifted one eyebrow as she posed a question. "Did something happen there?"

"No. All is well there. For now."

A sly smile crept onto her face. "But as you are probably aware, the people of this village do not like to speak of things that they fear, and sometime before your arrival, the water frosted over, causing the creatures that dwell there and in turn the villagers a lot of distress."

Amanda's cheeks warmed with her words, and she shifted uncomfortably on her feet as the quarter keeper continued.

"The pond had never frosted before and hasn't since. We should keep it that way."

The smile melted off the quarter keeper's face as she finished speaking, and Amanda tightened her grip on the staff again.

She tried to remain calm as she contemplated the idea that Kaelah knew who she was, or at the very least that she could have been the cause of the changes around the water.

She kept her words even as she pretended to disregard the suggestion. "Do you know where Howin and Dhruv are?"

The quartermaster huffed. "Your words and actions are not as subtle as you think they are. You should work at that." Kaelah righted herself. "I don't know, they just aren't here today. I was told to be and I am." She shrugged then added in a louder voice, "Keep quiet and get out of line if you have no desire for an assignment."

Footsteps approached from behind, and Amanda stepped to the side to allow the person to access Kaelah.

She watched in silence as Kaelah handed the tree-shaped brooch to them, along with a small parcel, then heard her say, "Be swift in your duties. I fear the visitor will arrive before the sun reaches its midday position."

Amanda furrowed her brow. *Maybe I wasn't as invisible as I believed.* She fidgeted while she thought, *If the quarter keeper meant me harm, she would have done something by now.*

As the volunteer left, another approached, but Kaelah turned to her and added, "Safe travels, Amana," and then made a shooing gesture with her hand in the same way Howin had the day before.

In a show of obedience, she moved farther away, then looked up at the sky to gauge the time. At best, she had a few short hours left before the celestial would show up. It was time to go.

Amanda heeded Kaelah's words and moved past the inlet before making her way deeper into the field between it and the tree line. She wasn't sure how far was far enough, but she had no desire to chance an encounter with the strange carnivorous plants that resided in the shadier areas.

Satisfied she was as far from the inlet as she could get, she reached for the dark magic inside her, knowing with the help of her staff, the long shadowy tendrils of energy would carry her back to the human realm.

<h1 style="text-align:center">19</h1>

Kiami - Troubling Sights

The Human Realm

Kiami was hesitant to call attention to the being that watched them. She had seen the young man in the returning light, soon after waking.

He was behind a tree a short distance away and pressing himself so close to the gnarled bark that if not for the outline of his clothing, he almost blended in. His hair looked to be the color of the forest floor shortly after dawn. It shined in the light and glittered as the last rays of sun caught speckles of dew that had formed there, as if he hadn't moved one centimeter from his position from sundown to sunup. It was the same young man that they were set to search for this morning.

She couldn't help but wonder if he was really who they had been looking for all along or if something else had slipped through the barrier of the realms, like the sorceress Bav that Tarah and Emily had described, or the three-headed monster, URD, that had attacked them in the Arcane realm. She tore her eyes away and looked into the fire.

Everyone else was at least pretending to still be asleep, and she doubted he would attack, since he hadn't already. The orange light of the remaining hot embers of their small fire flickered as if the glow would cease for good at any second.

Content to watch it struggle to keep burning, she decided not to try to stoke the flames. She doubted it mattered if she let it go out on its own. Justin had only started the fire to show Tarah one of his jinn-inherited talents. It hadn't been chilly, and it seemed the traveling show had done a good job of scaring the local wildlife away long before they had arrived.

Emily lifted her head from where she rested, then pushed herself up. Kiami watched in silence as her eyes darted around and she sucked in her breath.

Emily saw him too, yet she moved to sit by her side without speaking.

"Do you think he is like Abaddon, or us?" Kiami whispered, then turned to look at her.

Emily chewed at her lip and wrapped a curl around her finger tightly like she did when she was thinking. "I believe that there is a good chance he could be the missing one."

"I'm sorry I didn't think of that to begin with."

Emily shrugged and wrapped her arms around her midsection.

Concerned, Kiami asked, "Are you all right?"

"For now. I just... You know, I have to release it sooner than later. I'm glad I got a little rest, but I can feel it now. Like a ball of pain that just wants to break out from beneath my skin."

Kiami swayed sideways to give Emily's shoulder a light tap. "I noticed that you guys made some small changes to help the animals back there. "

Emily lifted her head and gave her a weak smile. "We did what we could. On closer inspection, they all seemed to be in good health. I don't think they were left unattended or caged up like that on a regular basis. And we hope that things go back to normal with the show now that Jasmine has lost control, whatever that means."

Kiami thought she heard something in her voice, as if she questioned her own actions. "Don't doubt yourself. You are doing great, Emily."

"Do you think I'm making the right choice taking Tarah with us?"

"I agree that we should not leave her here if she wants our help. Maybe Gemma can aid her after all this is over, if she is still in her current condition."

"She was quiet all night. I think she is having second thoughts."

"We all second-guess our choices sometimes."

"I feel responsible for her. I thought she was scared. I didn't tell her everything, but I told her a bit about the gems and how they amplify our powers, to put her mind at ease."

Across from where they sat, Kiami could see Justin and Etzion stirring. She focused her gaze back on Emily. "You did what you thought was best for her. What else could you do?"

Emily didn't respond, so Kiami nodded toward the others and said, "The boys are awake."

Then she glanced up at the forest's border. The young man had multiplied himself and spread out to form a line.

"And he," Kiami breathed out the words just as he began to advance, encircling their camp with his replicas as he did, "is making a move. Get ready."

Kiami hopped to her feet and shouted a reminder to the others. "I think his copies are like Aeron's. They are flesh and blood but move when he moves, similar to a mirror image of himself."

Emily stood up and spun in a circle as if she was inspecting the army before asking. "With Aeron, since he used wolves, it was easy to tell where he was. How do we know which one is him and which is a copy?"

"I'm not sure yet."

As Justin and Etzion joined them, Kiami caught a look of shock in the newer member's eyes.

Justin must have noticed it too, she thought, because she saw him give Etzion a light cuff on the shoulder as he quipped, "I hope you're a morning person."

Etzion smirked but squeaked out a reply. "Always."

"Where are our gems Em?" Justin asked.

"I left the bag by Tarah,"

Kiami searched the area with her eyes, but Tarah was suddenly nowhere to be seen. "She must be using the opal to stay hidden."

"You don't think she would leave with them, do you?" Emily asked with a hint of concern.

"Didn't you tell her about Jacob and how dangerous they are?"

"I wanted her to feel better, not worse!"

Justin shook his head. "I told you this whole thing was going too smooth."

"Okay, I have an idea. First things first, try to get him to talk, maybe we can tell where he is that way."

It was Justin who initiated the conversation, yelling, "We have been looking for you."

"What a coincidence, because I have been following you."

"Are you a half-blood, like us?" Etzion asked.

He shook his head but said, "Who knows?"

"Did someone send you?"

He ignored the question. "I want to see what you're all about, that's all."

"At least tell us your name," Etzion prodded.

"I am nobody."

Justin turned his face in her direction and whispered, "Well. Which one is it?"

"I can't tell!"

"We need to make a move before he does," he replied.

She thought she heard real concern creeping into Etzion's words as he asked in a low voice, "You think he can take us on by himself?"

Something had changed since the day before, when they had seemed to work so well together, and their lack of confidence coupled with Emily's made Kiami anxious.

"What has gotten into you guys?" she asked as she looked at each of them. When none of them made a response after a few seconds, Kiami ground her feet down, steadying herself as if bracing for impact. "That's it."

She knew her ability to control others with song would affect them as well, so she sent her party a warning. "I have had enough of this. Brace yourselves."

She pasted a smile on her face and focused her eyes on the many images of the young man. Then she pushed the song out and began to sway in time with it.

As his senses were invaded, he began to move with her, and she felt her own energy renew. Then his copies ceased their action and folded back in, overlapping with his original form as he again became one being.

When she ended her song, she hoped the others were ready. They would be stunned momentarily as they regained complete control of their senses, but they knew what to expect. She moved toward the young man and grabbed his arm, holding it in a tight grip. The young man did not try to yank away from her grasp as she would expect but instead looked up at her, pursing his lips, then furrowing his brow before speaking. "I was just having fun."

Justin produced a piece of rope from his supply pack and then rushed to her side to tie his hands together.

When the task was completed, he looked her in the eyes and whispered, "Was that really necessary?"

"None of you seemed to have a plan in mind," she murmured back.

She released their captive's arm and then raised her voice an octave as she added, "Could you check him for a gem, please?"

"Sure thing." He tore his eyes from hers, then pushed the captive a few feet away before he began his search.

Kiami furrowed her brow as she thought about following him to ask what he had been planning to do, but Etzion's exclamation stopped her.

"Wow!"

His eyes were as wide as saucers as he approached. "It's one thing to hear about your song, but to live it!"

Kiami blushed. "Thanks." No one had ever been so thrilled with her using her ability in their vicinity before; in fact, to her Justin seemed a bit annoyed with her for it. Feeling awkward about the compliment, she hesitated and raised one eyebrow at him. "I think."

She was glad when she heard Justin exclaim, "It's here!" removing Etzion's attention from her.

When she looked up at him in acknowledgment, Justin's burst of excitement evaporated as he added, "How will we stop him from multiplying? And causing more trouble?"

Kiami suggested, "Let's get him back to the jinn village. I think we need to hit reset before we do anything else.

Justin nodded toward her as if in agreement.

"He is out of control and will be unpredictable. It could be dangerous to travel with him," Etzion added, the enthusiasm gone from his voice.

"What would happen to him if the town barrier stops him?" Emily asked.

Kiami answered, "Then we take him to Justin's property outside of town until we feel that we can bring him there."

"Does anyone have something to cover his eyes with?" Justin asked, then continued to explain, "If he can't see what's happening, he may be more inclined to behave."

Etzion pulled a bandana from his pocket and waved it around like a flag. "How's this?"

"I think that'll do. Won't it, Justin?" Emily said, but she didn't sound relieved to Kiami.

She was reminded why as Justin and Etzion guided the blindfolded captive to where she and Emily stood, and Justin held up the orange stone he had found. "Now, we need to figure out where your red backpack is, Em."

She seemed to grow paler with his words. Then he asked, "Do you really think Tarah has it?"

Emily's face sank. "I left it with her."

Tarah reappeared then. "Yes, you did."

She held on to the backpack's straps with one hand. The main pocket hung open like a gaping mouth.

"I was just trying to keep the gems safe after you told me how important they were. I thought I was doing you a favor."

"You did." Emily took a hesitant step forward, then Tarah shook her head,

"I heard it all, Emily. You don't trust me. You thought I ran off with them!"

"I'm sorry. I didn't really mean it, Tarah. It's just that if the stones were gone, it would be another thing that's my fault."

"Funny you should say that. I heard what you said to her about Bav as well." Tarah moved one of her arms up and down. "Is this your fault?"

Kiami stepped forward. "No, what happened to you is not Emily's fault."

"Liars," she growled. "You know, my parents were right about one thing at least. Some people really are just better than others."

"We can still help you," Kiami insisted, but even as she spoke, Tarah thrust her three empty hands into the bag.

"In fact, I don't think you should have these at all."

Kiami heard Emily yell, "I want to help you. Don't do it!"

A pungent acidic smell wafted in her direction like a vinegar potpourri, as the young woman Emily desperately wanted to help lifted three gems from the bag at once, then tossed the pack behind her.

She heard her friend scream out at the sight, then Justin yell, "Drop them, Tarah. Before it's too late."

But Kiami knew she was already beyond saving.

She found it hard to look away, and yet that was the one thing she truly wanted to do.

When Emily talked about Jacob's end, she hadn't described to her the way his body must have been encapsulated by a glowing field of energy, as Tarah's was now.

Her flesh seemed to drip off her and pool beneath her body, like a light blue crayon would melt if held in the center of a flame.

She heard their blindfolded captive ask, "What is that smell?"

Her stomach twisted painfully at the sight, then her muscles con-tracted. She bent forward and dry-heaved, relieved to finally be free of the image, if only for a moment.

When Kiami lifted her face, it was over. All that remained beyond their own gems was the opal, as if the rest had seeped into the dirt below.

Their captive called out again, "What is happening?"

Justin muttered, "Nothing. Shut up."

Kiami made her way to the backpack and picked it up, then returned to the spot where Tarah had been to replace the gems. Once they were secure in the zipped bag, she bent down and picked up the now chainless opal.

She moved to the spot where Emily had sunk down to the ground. Her knees were pulled into her chest, and her back heaved up and down as she cried.

"Em," she said softly, "you had good intentions. Perhaps Tarah hadn't from the start."

"She seemed sincere," Emily whispered, her face still against her knees.

Kiami had thought so too. She raised a hand to her mouth and chewed at a nail, wondering if she had pushed Tarah over the edge when she used her voice. She hadn't even thought of Tarah and how she would react to something like that. She like the captive, hadn't known about her ability to control people with her song.

Kiami pulled her nail away from her teeth and raised the finger higher to inspect the ragged remains, then she dropped her hand to her side. Feeling a fresh wave of guilt wash over her, she cleared her throat and then added, "Well, maybe she was at first. People do strange and unpredictable things when they are scared. You know that." She hoped Justin would understand that she was addressing them both as she concentrated her efforts on Emily.

Emily lifted her face and wiped at her eyes with the back of her hand.

"You should have this," Kiami added as she held the opal out for her friend to take.

She reached toward it, then lightly grazed the stone with the tips of her fingers before retracting her hand.

"Will you hold on to it for me? For now, at least?"

"If that's what you want," Kiami answered as she knelt down in the grass beside her.

She put her arm around Emily's shoulder in an attempt to comfort her, then added, "I'm sorry, Em, but we have to go."

"I know," she answered, then lowered her face back down.

Justin and Etzion moved in closer with the multiplier between them, then the air became thick with the static energy of Etzion's magic.

20

Emily - Refuge

The Human Realm

This time, when Emily traveled with Etzion's help, she didn't get the feeling of nothingness that had taken over her senses, and she was relieved, although what had happened to Tarah still weighed on her.

She hadn't known the girl long, but she had taken it upon herself to claim responsibility for what had happened to her and had made a promise to help her.

Kiami removed her arm from her shoulder and stood up beside her, then bent down and offered her a hand.

Emily accepted the help, then wrapped her in a hug as she whispered thanks into her ear.

Kiami hugged her back then as she released her said, "It's no big deal. I told you we need to work together on all accounts, whether it's fighting a tangible monster or our own inner thoughts. At the end of the day, I know you will be there to pick me up, as I will you."

"On that note," Justin interrupted, "I know it's not what you want to hear, Em, but it seemed to me that Tarah hadn't changed as much as she thought she had. Better you found out now than later, don't you think?"

"You're both right," she said, "on all accounts, "but I still regret my decision to leave out the details of how dangerous the gems could be. Her life didn't need to end that way."

"Can I have my carnelian stone back now?"

Emily approached the young man to get a better look at him. His hair was twisted up against the back of his head by the blindfold, making it hard to see, but upon closer inspection, she noted thin strands of an orangey color mixed in and hidden with the rest of the sandy mess.

She glanced up at Justin. "Do you think we can safely remove the blindfold?"

"Are you going to try anything?" Justin asked.

He shook his head. "I was just goofing around. I wasn't going to hurt anyone."

"I wish we could believe that," Etzion said.

"Keep his hands bound behind his back for now, if it makes you feel better," Kiami offered, and Emily nodded.

Agitated, Justin pulled the bandana off without untying it.

"Geez, guy. Take it easy. I can't regrow body parts."

Emily's eyes locked onto his, and she noted the bright orange flecks that dotted his irises as he spoke again. "Marise. My name is Marise."

She turned away. "Can I see the stone, Justin?" She didn't want to say anything more until she was sure, just to be safe.

"Justin removed a cloth from his pocket and handed it to her. She could feel the weight of the stone hidden beneath the covering as she peeled it back, revealing a bright orange chunk of mineral stone.

She recovered the stone and turned to hand it to Kiami. "Could you put it with the rest for now?"

"Sure."

Emily took a deep breath and wondered how the scent of fire was still clinging to the air here. It felt to her like so much time had passed since the altercation with Aeron, yet one deep breath was all it took to remember how the house twenty yards from them had been ruined by the imposter's attack.

With the thought still lingering, she turned back to their captive to interrogate him. "So, Marise. Before we say anything or do anything we could live to regret, why don't you tell us why you were following us, and then explain why you would attack us."

He gave an awkward shrug. "I told you, I was just having fun. It was the will-o-the-wisps that led me to you in the beginning. I got bored following you around those tents. Then I spotted the owl there and hid."

He nodded in Kiami's direction. "I thought she would do a better job looking for me. But she gave up so fast."

"So Blaine led you to us?" Emily asked, her frustration building as her desire to release the pressure in her chest rose.

"Is that what you call the will-o-the-wisps in these parts?"

"Blaine's a person. Like you and me," she yelled back.

She felt Kiami's hand rest on her shoulder. "Steady, Emily. He probably never revealed himself to Marise either."

"I know, it's just..." She needed to release the pressure, but she couldn't get the words out.

The static in her ears increased, and she felt Kiami's hand move from her shoulder to her fingers, interlocking with them and then pulling her away.

Her free hand went to her throat as she allowed herself to be moved.

21

Amanda - Return

The Chaos Realm

Once Amanda felt the ground firmly beneath her feet, she opened her eyes and lifted them skyward, searching for signs that her use of the gem for transportation had further damaged the barrier between the realms.

But nothing in the immediate vicinity of Justin's house seemed out of place at first glance. Unsure if he had been successful in eliminating the prying eyes from the center of town, she had aimed for this familiar place instead of returning to Emily's sanctuary.

She moved toward the burned building, heading for the driveway. Despite his frequent distrust of her, she pitied Justin for what he had lost, but to her the house still looked savable, which was more than she could say for her own childhood home.

Jacob had made sure she would never be able to return to it, and she had stood by helplessly as it had collapsed from the damage he had caused while trying to get her under his thumb.

In all fairness, she thought as a smile spread on her face, *I would have a hard time trusting me, myself.*

As she neared the end of the driveway, three figures standing very close to one another came into view around the corner of the house. It was Justin, Etzion, and the boy she had seen in her visions that could multiply himself.

She paused, searching for Kiami and Emily, but they were nowhere within sight. She let out a relieved sigh. She wasn't sure how strong the signal would be with the six of them together, but she knew she needed time to explain, and she couldn't be sure what Kiami had told them about the mountain. Amanda knew she wasn't much for keeping secrets, and she could hold no ill will toward her if she had told them what she admitted to doing to her guardian.

She inhaled deeply, preparing herself for the possibility of attack, then moved around the side of the house toward the trio.

Amanda was almost sure she saw a smile plastered on Justin's face when she approached, as if he was happy to see her. But slowed her steps as she realized the third person with him was bound. The boy from her visions was their captive.

She tightened the grip on her staff as he bounded forward. "Amanda!"

Even though there was evident excitement in his approach and the tone of his voice, she couldn't bring herself to relax as she asked, "Why is he tied like that?"

A look of bewilderment flashed across his face as he stopped short of her at arm's length. "Marise?"

She gave one quick nod. She hadn't known his name. But it was clear that he spoke of the boy from her visions.

"He wasn't playing nice. I wouldn't think you would disapprove of his treatment. I thought you would be happy to know that I took care of that problem at the center of town..."

She cut him off. "Good."

She knew her comment sounded dismissive. But although she was somewhat relieved to hear Justin say he had solved the problem with the spying eyes, she needed to know where everyone was if she didn't want the celestial to come for them.

His shoulders dropped as if she had deflated him. "Kiami took Emily off in that direction," he said, pointing toward the tree line. "But who knows when Blaine will show up."

"Blaine?"

"Yeah, the last piece of the puzzle. The seventh," he added with renewed vigor, as if his excitement had been restored by the very idea that he had useful information for her.

"Where is this Blaine?"

Justin raised a hand and pushed the hair back away from his eyes nonchalantly before he spoke. "Who knows? Blaine is the wisps; the wisps are Blaine."

His eyes twinkled as he made the announcement, and Amanda felt the blood drain from her face. She knew if Blaine and the wisps were the same person, he could appear at any moment and compromise everything.

"Someone needs to go. I don't have time to explain." She didn't bother masking the urgency in her voice.

"Slow down," Etzion said. He had come closer, pulling Marise by the arm.

"There isn't time to slow down. I can't chance the celestial finding us all together. I have given up too much to make sure I see this through for it to end now."

Given the fact that Justin hadn't come at her with anger in his eyes, she doubted Kiami had told him everything she had said on the mountain. *Perhaps*, she thought, *it should stay that way a little longer.*

She looked up and locked her eyes onto Etzion's. He looked frightened, and as she opened her mouth, he took a step back again, dragging his captive with him.

"Can you take Justin with you to your home? I know where it is, and I can send Kiami with a message when the time is right."

He gave her a slow nod.

"What about him?" he asked, glancing sideways at Marise.

"Leave him, take him, it's up to you two. Whatever you can handle. Just go."

Justin stepped in front of her. "Not until you tell us why."

"I'm just trying to keep us alive that much longer."

He crossed his arms over his chest, reminding her of how she had responded to the goddess's demands.

"Okay, okay. When all the stones are together, they emit a unique frequency that the celestial can pinpoint. Get it?"

"See, now that wasn't so hard. And without that information, sending us away would have been pointless. Emily has most of our gems right there. In that backpack."

"Thanks."

"No problem," he said as he reached for the bag Emily had left behind. He opened it and retrieved his jade gem then stuffed it into his pocket.

"Etzion, let's leave Marise with her. I need a vacation anyway."

In response, he swiveled his head to look from Justin at her then asked, "You will be in contact?"

"Yes, as soon as I catch Kiami and Emily up." She nodded over at Marise then added, "Him too. Everyone needs to know exactly what's coming."

Amanda flinched as Etzion held up his stone then moved toward Justin as he asked, "You ready?"

She had forgotten that he needed to use it to transport more than just himself. She doubted all the evidence of her own trip had cleared yet. With two uses of the stones within such a short time and small area, she could only hope the repercussions wouldn't be more than they could handle.

When the pair had stepped away and vanished from her sight, she loosened her grip and let her shoulders slump. She hadn't been expecting to find they had been in contact with both the missing half-bloods.

She sighed and looked at the young man she knew only from random visions. She didn't really think he posed a threat, not from the few interactions she had witnessed. He had seemed to be a loner, always practicing his gift with no one around and always wearing some obscure band t-shirt and holey jeans.

"Marise, is it?"

He gave a nod.

She searched her memory for the familiar name. "One who is infinite, endless. That seems fitting."

As she moved to untie his hands, she added, "Listen, I know what you can do. You aren't familiar with me, but I have seen you in action plenty of times."

Once the rope was untied, she offered her hand. "I'm Amanda."

He took it and responded, keeping his voice flat, "A pleasure, I'm sure."

She picked up Emily's red backpack and hoisted it onto her shoulder. "Well, then. That's that. Come with me." She motioned for him to follow, then spun on her heels toward the town.

As he caught up to walk beside her, she explained, "The girls won't have any trouble finding us when they are ready, and there are a few things I missed in the human realm while I was away. Now that I am here, I am eager to get back to them."

"You were in another realm, beyond this one?"

"You know about them?"

His steps slowed as he answered, "Blaine told me some things."

She stopped for a moment and turned to face him. "I would be interested in finding out more about that conversation, but first I would love to hear what you did that got everyone so bent out of shape. I mean, it doesn't take much to get Justin going, but Etzion, Emily, and Kiami? It must have been some show you put on."

She gave him a wide smile, then turned back and continued toward the town. She became so engrossed in his tale that she barely noticed the strange hum that was carried on the wind from the direction they had come from.

22

Kiami - Abominable

The Human Realm

Kiami made a beeline for the woods, pulling Emily behind her. Only about thirty yards beyond the tree line, everything had changed.

What was once a lush forest ended in an abrupt line in back of them. In front of her, patches of sand and snow dotted a clearing that went on as far as her eyes could see. She stopped in her tracks and released Emily's hand. The air here was thick with the feeling of a coming storm, and she was reminded of her time in this same forest with Emily when the small dragons had appeared.

At her feet was a smooth-looking creature of about seven inches long. It peered up at her from its place in a snowy mound, lifting its four appendages in her direction, revealing its suction-cupped fingers.

"A grindyliz," she said in shock. She had seen one in the Arcane realm, and Aden had told her the creature didn't belong there.

She reached down to pick up the animal and allowed it to crawl to her shoulder. Aden had referred to it as a blood-sucking symbiotic critter, so when she felt a pinch on her flesh, she shrugged it off. He had also said it was intelligent, and she could use all the help she could get.

A loud buzz sounded overhead, and she lifted her face to the sky. Above her, the noise escalated by the second. The wind kicked up, blowing her dark hair into her face, and she looked on as a helicopter appeared out of nowhere, hovering above them like it was stuck in place. The sky behind it shimmered like the sun rising on a rippling lake.

She felt Emily grasp her hand as the door was flung open and a ladder unfurled over the side. Kiami gave it a light squeeze as she watched on while someone stepped out onto the ladder one foot at a time. She couldn't make out if it was a man or a woman, just the form of a two-legged creature clinging and slowly maneuvering toward the ground.

Emily's grip tightened as Kiami stared. The figure hesitated, then leapt. The face contorted, but she couldn't tell if the person was screaming or saying something as they plummeted toward them.

She couldn't hear anything above the noise that was emanating from the machine as she watched, stunned by the events.

A lightning-fast movement from behind the ladder caught her eye before she could react to the figure's leaping form, and she realized the body had abandoned the safety of the rope and wood to stay out of the thing's reach.

She screamed at the top of her lungs. "There, Emily. Up there!"

She pointed to the long, white, cylindrical thing that reached out from beyond the rippling sheen, grasping for the ladder with its spade-shaped appendage, just as another figure appeared from inside the open door. This second passenger didn't even attempt to use the ladder but instead leapt feet-first to their inevitable doom.

The creature was ready, and Kiami watched on, horrified, as another strange appendage shot out from behind the shimmer and snatched it out of thin air as it fell, then pulled its treasure through to whatever realm its body was in.

The second appendage shot back through, reaching out and wrapping itself around the machine. As it did, Kiami saw the propellers slow, then stop. The buzzing was replaced by an incredible crunching noise that seemed to echo back at her from her place on the ground.

She rotated to face Emily, unsure if she would be able to hear her over the hum of her own magic trying to escape. "Hit that thing before it decides to come all the way through."

To her relief, Emily nodded and took a few steps forward, then released the wave of her magic toward the thing.

A sharp screech followed, and Kiami lifted her hands to her ears as she spun back.

The tentacle gripping the ladder released its hold, then retracted behind the sheen. The other loosened and went limp. Kiami pivoted her body around again and yelled, "Run."

When she made it back behind the tree line, Kiami wrapped her arms around one of the trunks, bracing herself for the impact just as the helicopter and the severed tentacle landed on the ground. The earth groaned as it shifted with the sudden addition of weight.

She thought she heard the familiar flurry of panicked wings, then another screech sounded from the distance, but it seemed as if it was muffled and fading more by the second.

Kiami let go of the trunk and sank into the dirt. She took a few steadying breaths, then called out, "Emily? Em?"

Her friend shot up from behind a fallen log a few feet away from her. "Here. I'm right here."

"Was that another rift?"

"I think it was more than one, or there have been several there within a short amount of time." Emily moved closer. "Because of the patches of sand and snow?"

"And the grindyliz," Kiami added, pushing herself back to her feet, then glancing at the critter on her shoulder."

"And the helicopter? Do they exist in other realms?"

"They might... Well, theoretically, the rifts would be happening all over, right?"

"I guess."

"What if someone in the human realm was curious and entered a rift, got stuck, and exited another when it appeared?"

"It would be possible... That's kind of what happened to Bav, and Bloise did say humans had seen things they couldn't unsee. Perhaps their curiosity got the better of them. We could go back and ask," said Emily.

"I'm not sure they could have survived that fall. But we should inspect before we return to the others."

They went to the clearing and then moved ahead toward the ruined helicopter, taking measured steps. Kiami's eyes darted back and forth from the sky to the ground. She wasn't surprised to see the rift had closed; she just wasn't sure whether or not another would tear open.

The creature's limp appendage lay out on the ground in a long curve. To Kiami, the shaggy limb appeared to be at least four meters in length.

"What the heck?" Emily tapped the side of it with her foot.

"An abominable," Kiami answered. Then stepped back.

Emily tilted her head to the side. "What?"

Kiami looked at the creature on her shoulder and patted its head lightly. "The grindyliz..." She paused, then added, "It is feeding me information on the creature."

Emily lifted her eyebrows in disbelief, so Kiami made an attempt to explain. "It's not speaking to me. It's showing me, in my mind."

"I think I get it. What else did it show you?"

"I will try to describe it. The abominable is from the cold realm where the grindyliz lives. It has several of these flexible limbs coming out of its backside and four legs with paws." She looked up into Emily's eyes and added, "Kind of looks like a giant white cat with wings.

Emily smirked. "And let's not forget those extra prehensile limbs. I think I get the picture. But I'm not sure I like the sound of it."

"It wouldn't like it here, too warm," Kiami added, then blushed. "Sorry. It's kind of odd. The way it shares information. Caught me off guard."

Kiami walked around the crushed helicopter, then made a wider circle, noting the pattern of debris as she moved. She was sure that there were no signs of humanoid beings, living or otherwise, to be found in the area.

"Em, we aren't going to find them. We should get back."

Emily seemed distracted. She had been staring hard at the ground in front of her feet as she followed. Now, she looked up and asked, "Why do you say that? You are usually such an optimist."

Kiami smiled. "I suppose I am."

She threw another glance at the symbiotic creature on her shoulder, wondering if the idea had been put in her head or if it had truly been her own.

Emily gave her a crooked smile and then placed her hands on her hips as she waited for the explanation.

"Okay, okay. I see a lot of things fall from the sky. I mean, I can fly." She shrugged, then pointed at some of the scattered remnants. "The debris that landed is all arched toward the tree line, and there's none on the other side of the helicopter, farthest from the tree line."

She watched as Emily reached for one of her dark curls, then wrapped it around her finger. "So you think anything that should have landed on that side of the helicopter went to the other realm?"

"Exactly."

"Okay." Emily released the curl and dropped her hand back to her side. "Let's go then. There was a lot of commotion over here."

She paused, shuffling her feet. "The helicopter was loud. I mean, I'm wondering why or how they didn't hear what was happening. We aren't that far away, and if there's been more than one rift, who's to say something else didn't come through?"

Kiami furrowed her brow. She hadn't even thought about that.

23

Amanda - Almost Rejoined at the Hip

The Human Realm

They moved through the barrier to town without any effort. To her surprise, when she and Marise neared the house they had been staying in after Justin's had become uninhabitable, Fizzle greeted her with several enthusiastic yelps.

Although much friendlier than Howin and Dhruv, Fizzle caused her to think of the pair. Like them, he was a little dangerous, but he was also fiercely loyal and protective of those he saw as friends.

She paused for a brief moment to greet him, patting the top of his head.

When she righted herself and continued toward the door, the fuzzy little monster ran circles around them on his short legs as they advanced with the end of his tongue hanging loose from his wide mouth.

He jumped up and down in front of the door when she turned the handle, and Amanda thought it was funny, considering he could have teleported through it, so she blocked him as she pushed it open, taking a moment to scold him before allowing him access. "Fizzle. Stop that."

"Fizzle? What is he?" Marise asked.

She propped her staff against the wall and let the backpack slide from her shoulder. It made a soft thump sound when it landed on the floor inside the entranceway as she attempted to answer.

"Yeah, he's, well, a teleporting critter?" she said, slightly unsure of her own words. Amanda didn't know which realm the species resided in or if the ability he had to move through them was a fluke brought on by the weakening of the barriers, but he seemed to have a knack for it.

"There is more to that monster than meets the eye. You will see. Just don't let him lick you," she went on with a mischievous grin.

As she made her way into the kitchen, as if in hindsight she added, "Or maybe you should."

The little creature ran up behind her as she opened the refrigerator door, and when she reached in, he began to dance at her feet.

Amanda pulled out an apple to feed the omnivore and then held it up in the air above him. Marise had followed her into the kitchen, and she watched his reaction as Fizzle opened his mouth all the way and shot his frog-like tongue up to take the treat she offered.

His eyes widened in surprise, and she shrugged at him then turned back to the fridge for a carbonated beverage as she addressed him again, adding, "He really is a delight."

She meant it, but she was trying to gauge Marise's reactions. When Kiami and Emily returned, she needed him willing to listen. She didn't have time to waste on disbelief or shock.

She took a sip of her drink and then asked, "Thirsty?"

He nodded, and she grabbed a second beverage before moving to the table to sit. When he didn't follow, she slid the drink across from her and motioned for him to join her. As he pulled out a chair to sit, she said, "Tell me about Blaine."

"The will-o-the-wisps," he started, pausing to take a gulp from his own drink, "or just wisps, according to your friends, has shown up from time to time along my path."

He looked up at her as if expecting something, and she offered, "It was the same for me and the others."

"I wanted to make sure you didn't think I was off my rocker." He looked back down at his drink.

He seemed unsure of himself, so Amanda tried to make light of what he said by saying, "Well, I don't know you well enough to make that determination in general, but about the wisps, I believe you."

He lifted the corners of his mouth then moved his lips back into a thin line. "I have been on my own for a while. Sometimes they brought me things to get by."

Amanda wasn't getting far, so she tried to soothe him more. It wasn't her forte, she knew, but she gave it a shot. "I am sorry to hear that. I mean, we have all had problems, us half-bloods. But how did Blaine go about introducing himself?"

"Well, a few days ago a swarm of wisps appeared. I mean, only one or two had even shown themselves to me at a time before that. It was like a swarm of bees. It startled me at first. Then they began to meld together and take form."

He reached up and scratched at his head, then brought his eyes to meet hers, and Amanda let out a sigh. She was going to have to lead him in the conversation.

"So, this form was human?"

"Human-like. It had a head and a body, arms, legs, but the facial features remained undefined, even after speaking."

"Okay," Amanda said as she lifted her drink and took a sip before going on. "So what did Blaine speak about?"

"I had been in an alley, reading a flyer for the traveling show. Blaine said I needed to go. If I did, I would find others with abilities like mine, and answers."

"And you just went?"

"The wisps had always helped me before. Having them morph into a human-like form, it stunned me, but I didn't have a reason not to believe. So, I went."

He nodded toward the entrance. "The wisps are the ones that showed me where the orange gem was, even before I chose to leave my home."

"So you know nothing about your gem or those I refer to as the half-bloods?"

He shook his head and looked back down. "I didn't really know the will-o-the... I mean, Blaine's name, until Emily said it earlier."

Amanda raised one of her brows. "So, the wisps didn't actually introduce themselves?"

Marise responded without looking up. "I guess Blaine only said what he needed to."

Amanda crinkled her nose at the declaration, then took a long drink and allowed herself to savor the refreshing tingle. She thought it was odd that Blaine would manifest his human form and not give his name, but then again, the half-blood had never even attempted to make an introduction with her, so she decided it was best to leave it alone for now. She had a lot to explain even before the girls got back.

As she dredged up the memories of where her own journey began, she felt a pang in her chest, but she knew her own story would offer a straightforward explanation of the things she had learned of this world that were most important to Marise's understanding.

"I didn't know anything about magic or the realms until I was fifteen." She started her tale and reminded herself that she didn't need to tell him everything.

Her mouth felt hot and dry, but as she brought her refreshment back up to her lips, she found she had finished the beverage. She looked down at the empty can and sighed.

She had been sipping on it nonstop as she told Marise about the day she had found the strange artifact in the woods that she would come to learn was the jinni Erol's prison, and how after finding it the sorcerer Jacob had pursued and kidnapped her, then deceived her by coercing her into helping him look for a ring that he was never actually after.

She skipped over many of the gritty details about her time in the Arcane realm while she was imprisoned, and instead focused on how she and Aden had managed to gain their freedom. Afterward, she summed up the tale by reiterating the myth of the world for his benefit.

Amanda fidgeted with the empty can. She would have liked to have another, but Fizzle had curled up near her feet beneath the table, and she didn't want to disturb him.

"Do you have any questions?"

Marise had seemed to be listening dutifully, and although he never interrupted her during the story, she was sure he had to have a few, but he only shook his head.

"Are you sure you understand?"

"I do. I mean, I'm not going to say I fully get all this realm stuff, but the concept, sure. I mean, it sounds like you had a rough time."

Fizzle made a sudden movement, darting toward the door, and Amanda glanced around the corner as she rose to replace her empty can.

When she didn't see him near the entrance, she assumed he had teleported out to meet Kiami and Emily as they made their way to the house.

After swallowing half of the cool drink, she moved back to the table and fell into the chair. "We all possess stories of how we got to this point. Mine began with a desire to find my mother after I learned she wasn't human."

Amanda thought of the mountain and the painful fact that her mom had known the celestial's plan all along. She added, "But the things we have uncovered since make me almost glad that I didn't know her well. I didn't really piece much of it together until I found Emily and Kiami."

Marise pulled his hands from the tabletop and moved them below it before looking up at her. "How did you find them?"

She offered him a vague explanation. "The visions I mentioned, which started during my time in the Arcane realm, led me to Emily and Kiami."

"So you had visions of me too?"

"I did, but not many. I mainly saw you practice your gift, not much more. So," she added in an attempt to change the direction of the conversation, "what's your story?"

Marise shrugged again. "I left on my own, and it sounds like I made the right choice. My parents, or whoever they were, really weren't bad or anything. Once I found I could multiply myself, I just knew somehow it wouldn't be good to tell them or be around them. I mean, it's not normal, and I didn't want anything to happen to them because of me."

Amanda lifted an eyebrow; she didn't quite buy it. The tale of Blaine was acceptable, but when coupled with the way he was generalizing all his responses, the story felt off. She thought about saying as much but relented.

She couldn't help her skepticism, and if something had happened to his guardians, as it had her own father, she could understand if he felt guilty and didn't want to acknowledge whatever it was. He clearly didn't want to talk about it now, so she decided to let it go, sure that whatever it was he was leaving out would come to light before long.

Instead, she shrugged back at him as if she was indifferent. She could already hear Emily and Kiami as they made their way up the steps and onto the porch anyway.

She removed her own hands from the tabletop and wrung them together on her lap. She could only hope that Kiami would be glad to see her.

24

Emily - Disapproving Fizzle

The Human Realm

When Fizzle ran up to meet them on the road, not far from the house, Emily felt a rush of relief at the fact that he was the only realm-hopping thing they had come across since they left the woods.

They hadn't waited long at Justin's before heading toward the sanctuary of the jinn town, but they took their time as they made their way to the house, watching the sky more intently the closer they got, looking for any signs of another tear or breech in the protective barrier that concealed the other realms.

Given that they encountered no trouble along their route, the fact that the trio wasn't where they had left them didn't worry her that much. Although she did plan to chastise them for causing her and Kiami anxiety in the first place when she got back to the house.

As she and Kiami paused to greet the fuzzy monster, Emily thought Kiami looked pleased that he had appeared, although Fizzle didn't seem very happy about the grindyliz she carried with her. When Kiami reached down to pet him, he growled at the lizard-like animal the moment he noticed it clinging to her shoulder.

As her friend rebuked and shushed him, Emily wondered if the little monster was right to be agitated. To her, Kiami's reaction time and possibly even her responses seemed to be affected when the creature shared information with her, and Emily had to wonder whether the shift would get worse with time.

Of course, she had to admit that interacting with Fizzle himself was not entirely harmless, since his saliva caused mood-altering effects due to a need to subdue prey. Given that insight, she knew it was possible that the grindyliz had no idea of the repercussions of his symbiotic relationship.

Although she did pity the displaced creature for being torn from his home, Fizzle's mistrust only fortified her doubts in regard to the matter. The fuzzball hadn't liked Aeron, after all, and he had been an imposter.

She wanted to test her theory.

Thinking that the creature could affect Kiami's responses, Emily didn't want to ask outright, so instead she posed another question that had occurred to her while Kiami tried to coddle a reluctant Fizzle.

"Kiami, what happens to that lizard thing if you change form, you know, all the way to an owl?"

A thoughtful look settled onto Kiami's face as she stood upright. "I'm not sure."

Her nose crinkled and her brow furrowed, as if a conversation was happening that Emily couldn't hear, then she asked, "Are you willing to take him?"

Emily crossed her arms over her chest. "No thanks."

She had no intention of finding out what hosting it would be like.

"I couldn't just leave it there. I don't think it would survive on its own in our realm long without help," Kiami reasoned.

"I know," Emily admitted, "and we will find an alternate solution.

I just … wonder." She shook her head. "Never mind. Let's get to the house. We can only deal with one thing at a time."

As Emily moved along the driveway and then made her way up the stairs, she heard a muffled voice coming from within, but it wasn't Justin's or Etzion's.

Given Kiami's state when she had returned from the mountain, Emily thought it would be best if she forewarned her. Kiami was a few paces behind, and she stopped then turned to face her before letting the words slip from her mouth. "She's back."

Fizzle was close at her heels, and as she made an abrupt stop, the little monster hit the back of Kiami's legs, then took several steps away from her and shook himself.

His reaction reminded her of how Kiami had shaken herself after leaving the main tent at the traveling show, as if the action would help her regain her sense.

A light giggle escaped Emily's mouth at the sight, and she quickly covered her lips with her hand before she whispered, "Poor Fizzle."

She lifted her eyes back up to where Kiami stood, then dropped her hand back at her side.

"I'm sure he's fine," Kiami whispered, paused, then continued in the same hushed tone, "Are you sure she's here?"

"Pretty sure it's her. Who else could it be?"

Emily watched as Kiami's face went slack, then a smile emerged, and she said, "Well, why are we waiting out here then?"

Her friend moved toward and past her on the steps before she could even turn around, and Emily quickly followed her inside.

25

Emily - Here and Now

The Human Realm

Both Marise and Amanda looked up from their seats at the table as she and Kiami entered the kitchen, and she found herself struck motionless in the moment as contentment washed over her at the sight.

Even though she had warned Kiami of the voice she heard from the outside and had seen Amanda's mud-caked staff as she entered, until that moment her return had not seemed entirely real.

Emily surveyed the room. Whatever they had been talking about, Marise's face looked tense with his mouth pulled in tight, as if his lips were pressed against his teeth.

Fizzle had made his way under the table, and he lay curled up near Amanda's feet, with one tiny eye half open to keep watch.

Amanda's eyes had grown wide, and she looked unsure of how to proceed, as if stricken speechless by the fact that Kiami had rushed forward and then bent down to give her an enthusiastic hug.

It was clear to Emily that she had not been expecting such a warm greeting.

After a brief pause, Amanda maneuvered the upper half of her body to return the embrace, even as a flush crept up her neck and cheeks. Then, as Kiami's grip loosened, her own face scrunched and she backed up a step as she asked, "What happened to your arm?"

Amanda winced at the question, and Emily tore her gaze from the pair, realizing she had been staring.

She made her way around them, then pulled out the chair at the far end of the table to take a seat. From her new vantage point, she could see the arm in question, and she agreed, the appendage looked off, almost as if a thin layer of bark had been applied over her skin.

"After you left me at the river," Amanda repositioned herself to face the table then continued matter-of-factly, "I found the celestial. My arm was taken, then gifted back as it is now."

"I'm glad you are here," Kiami crooned.

"Likewise." Amanda folded her hands in front of her. "But where did you find your friend?"

Kiami shot her a quizzical look and asked, "Marise?"

"No, the grindyliz."

"Oh... I forgot he was there, honestly," Kiami whispered so low, it was as if she was speaking to herself.

Emily cleared her throat. "He was in a small mound of snow, beyond the woods, near Justin's family home."

Kiami's eyes brightened, as if she had just remembered something. "Oh yes, it was strange. There weren't just signs that a rift had leaked things in from his realm, but others as well."

Amanda shook her head. "I was afraid of something like that happening after I sent Justin and Etzion away."

Emily groaned. "You sent them away? We only just returned from finding Marise."

Amanda gave a quick nod then looked down at her hands. "It's a complicated story. Maybe you two should fill me in on what you have been up to before I explain. Marise here has already told me about his part in it."

Emily cast her gaze on him. She thought he looked more relaxed, so she addressed him. "It's nice to meet you, Marise. I'm sorry about the precautions we took and for rushing off. But it was necessary."

His eyes lifted to meet hers. "Don't worry about me. I'm just taking it all in. Forget I'm here."

She cocked her head to the side. "Do you need anything?"

One corner of his mouth lifted in a slight smile. "No. But thank you."

She acknowledged him with a weary smile, then focused her attention back on Kiami and Amanda as she wondered where to begin.

Emily tugged at one of her curls and started twisting it around her finger. "First off, don't ever do that to me again. Either of you."

She looked back and forth from Amanda to Kiami. "Taking off like that and leaving me with only Justin for company. I like him and all, but when there is absolutely no one else around to pass time with in this ghost town, he can be a bit much."

"He just needs a project to keep him focused," Kiami offered as she finally pulled a chair out to join them at the table.

"True. He didn't waste any time coming up with a solution to stop those spying eyes. But I didn't know what was happening to either of you. Justin told me about the mountain and how Kiami insisted on following you, but I was worried."

Amanda's shoulders stiffened, and her eyes seemed to harden with each word. "I was trying to keep you all away for your own protection while I could. I don't regret it."

Emily sighed; she wasn't trying to get under Amanda's skin. She needed to make that clear. "It's evident that a lot went on up there, but here, time seemed to slow down, I swear. Then there was Jacob. He showed up at Justin's outside of town."

She paused and released a shallow breath, then spoke quickly. "I don't want to scare Marise, but I think it's best that he knows."

Amanda seemed to breathe her words through clenched teeth. "He is aware of my history with Jacob."

Emily released her curl, then folded her hands in front of her. "Before I knew what was happening, he picked up all the stones at once."

Amanda's eyebrows lifted. "He's gone for good then?"

Curious, Emily asked, "Did you know what would happen?"

"No. I mean, I knew only we could handle them. I had seen the evidence like you had, that they harmed those that weren't like us if held for a short time without some kind of layer of protection."

"Unfortunately, he wasn't the only one that was hurt by them while you were gone, but that was later ... after Etzion returned."

She continued, "When Kiami got back, she needed time to recuperate, but she filled us in on what we *needed* to know. By then, for me, the pull to leave here was already strong, and it became worse by the day. I did my best to do what you asked. To take charge."

"Given that you found Marise and Blaine, it would seem like you did exactly that."

Emily shrugged. She didn't feel like she had. "We spent a lot of time prepping for travel and did a little research, but we didn't know who we were looking for, so when Etzion showed up and said he thought he had a lead, we jumped at the chance. Perhaps a little too eagerly."

Amanda leaned forward, her interest piqued. "What do you mean?"

26

Amanda - Mistaken Identity

The Human Realm

The warm welcome Kiami had given her, coupled with the way Emily had stressed the word "needed" when she spoke about Kiami's update after her return, left Amanda to assume that she had kept certain parts about her time on the mountain to herself and that Emily was well aware she didn't know everything that had transpired.

She shook her head at the latest piece of information, but it was Marise who spoke up; having only just heard her tale of how she disposed of the guardian in the void between the realms, the information was still fresh in his mind.

"That was a bad idea!"

"Etzion said he didn't think it mattered because we were not going from realm to realm," Emily reasoned.

Amanda shook her head. "Justin was right to be angry. There is a place, like a pocket of empty space between the barriers, and it is not that difficult to end up there."

As she said it out loud, she wondered, what would happen to that lost guardian if the realms did come down? Would he free himself and be the first to seek her in order to exact revenge for his imprisonment? She doubted he would take pity on her naivety at the time.

"We found something else before we discovered Marise."

"I think it was *me* that discovered *you*," he quipped.

Emily folded her arms over her chest. "Well, it's the reason we acted so hastily when you pulled your stunt back there, so maybe you should listen."

Amanda smirked at her. "Go on."

"Etzion brought us to this traveling show because he thought he had found a half-blood. But he had actually found a young woman whom had been cursed by none other than Bavmordia."

"The sorceress you encountered before you found the jinn town?"

"Exactly. From Tarah's story, it sounded like Bav had slipped through a breach in the barrier. When she didn't get to fulfill her desire to teach, after my escape she found her as a replacement. Her curse or lesson was to be transformed into the monster she acted like."

Amanda said knowingly, "And I bet you felt responsible."

"Yes. Well, we were. Even if inadvertently."

When her words sank in, Amanda beamed as she thought, *The goddesses were wrong. I am not as much of an anomaly as they think.*

"Was Bav with her?"

"No, they got separated. A tear appeared, and a tentacled creature pulled Bav back through with it. Tarah said when it happened, she caught hold of the chain of her opal, and when it came free, Bav aged rapidly, so I don't think she will ever get another chance to teach again."

The image of the tentacled creature that attacked them during their first visit to the Chaos realm invaded her mind, and Amanda sat back in her chair as she remembered the large leather boots and the human-esque bones they had discovered nearby before the plant-like creature had attacked.

She agreed, "I think you're right. So, Tarah had the opal?"

"Bav had told her that the curse would go away once she learned her lesson, so when she met someone at the show that she thought could benefit from it, she gave it to them."

Amanda wasn't surprised by the story. It seemed to her that Tarah had about as much luck as they had in their dealings with people from other realms, so she voiced her assumption. "Let me guess, it backfired?"

"Pretty much. She was imprisoned and hurt. I healed her before we let her out of her literal cage, and right after, the woman she tried to help, Jasmine, showed up."

"You guys were very busy."

"She wasn't hard to deal with, not really. But the situation kept compounding. We set out to bring Tarah back with us. I thought that she could join us here and start over as I did." She gulped audibly, as if she was losing a battle with her emotions.

"But then Marise showed up and things got out of control. Tarah freaked out. I guess she couldn't handle everything. She tried to take the gems, not understanding how dangerous it was."

By the way Emily's eyes now glistened with tears, Amanda knew it hadn't ended well for her.

Marise must have understood where the story was going as well because he squeaked out an apology. "Emily, I'm sorry. I didn't mean for anyone to get hurt."

Kiami spoke up shakily. "No. You're not the only one to blame. I deserve some of it. And I should have said something sooner. Tarah wasn't ready when I used my song. Like you, Marise, she had no idea how it would affect her. I acted rashly."

Stricken by the confession, Amanda moved her eyes over Kiami. Whether she had requested the lizardlike creature to do so or it had decided to of its own accord, it had released itself from her shoulder and now lay on the tabletop with its eyes closed as if it were napping.

Emily wiped at her wet cheeks with one hand. "It's okay. I have moved past it. I know it doesn't do any good to dwell on what-ifs, and none of you should either."

Without missing another beat, she picked up her retelling where she had left off. "Once we got back, the opposing energy from healing Tarah was trying to force its way out.

"That is why Kiami took me into the woods to release the energy, like you had before. When we stumbled upon the place where the tears had occurred, we found much more than just the grindyliz, but we dealt with it. And I guess that brings us back to here and now, for me at least," Emily concluded.

Kiami looked up into her eyes. "Emily left out the fact that Justin had a kind of epiphany while you were gone, and he told us about the history of the tree at the center of town. It seems that the tree can be used as a conduit to get to the Emerald Mountains."

Amanda flashed her a worried smile of understanding. Kiami meant to try to go there to get Jacqueline.

As much as she would prefer to leave the scorned jinni where she was, she nodded at Kiami and said, "I could see now how that could be helpful."

"I was torn by what you said at the river. But as I waited to regain my strength, the wisps visited me. When they merged together and became Blaine, we spoke of many things. "

"You can say it, Kiami. I'm not afraid of what I did. Not anymore."

Kiami shook her head.

"I will then. I banished your guardian to the jinn realm."

"You probably saved her life."

"Perhaps," Amanda admitted, letting her shoulders droop as she looked over at Emily, whose mouth hung open in a way that suggested she had no idea, and as their eyes met, she snapped it closed.

"Is there anything else, Kiami?"

"I stayed close by until after the mountain fell. I shouldn't have. Blaine warned me against it. But I was worried about you."

"Yes, well, what did you see?"

"After the collapse, I found strange debris around the site. I brought some back with me, but Justin couldn't determine what the pieces were from."

Amanda gave her a nod. Justin didn't know what they were, but she had an idea.

"As I collected them, I got the feeling something was watching me, and I knew it wasn't you or Blaine, so I guess I kind of left in a hurry."

"It could have been the celestial returning. He wasn't at the mountain when it fell."

Kiami gave a slow nod and then asked, "Where did you go after?"

"I went to the Chaos realm to find his daughters." She let out a haggard sigh before continuing. "The celestials are very real," she started, thinking of the words the imprisoned parents had used. "That's why we are here. Trapped, being punished for a movement against them."

Amanda tried not to sound overly ominous. She hoped to avoid going into too much detail as she addressed the facts. "You need to understand what I found out first. Before I traveled to the Chaos realm, I learned that our genetic parents with abilities were in on his plan all along. They were made willing to play a part through threats and promises. Many of them relented once we were born, which is why several of you have never met either of your real parents and never will."

"Like me?" Emily questioned, and Amanda nodded in her direction.

"I believe Etzion was taken in by replacement parents as well," she added.

She couldn't undo what she had done, and until the celestial was gone, dredging it up would only further separate her from the others at the one time they had to be united, no matter what. Although she knew it could and most likely would end up coming out at some point, throwing a new wrench into the cogs.

Realizing she was going to need more allies, Amanda sucked in a breath. "The point is, we are still just pawns. All of us. Even you, Kiami, are not immune to the manipulation of the celestial and his daughters. Which is why I think we should work to retrieve Jacqueline, sooner rather than later."

Shock contorted Kiami's features, and as she moved to push herself up from her chair, Amanda motioned for her to remain seated.

"Don't celebrate just yet. First, you should keep in mind that she may not be very happy to see me, and second, I haven't explained the whole situation."

As Amanda began to tell the tale of the underground lair she had visited, she was determined to describe every detail, including the wall of twinkling lights that had appeared and how during their conversation her anger had almost gotten the best of her, more than once.

"At least part of the pull we feel toward each other is the gems trying to reunite."

Emily's face became wrinkled with lines of worry, and Amanda soothed her. "I'm glad you kept them together and close. It was the right call at that time."

She turned her head to look each of them in the eye, then added, "Now is a different story."

As she finished explaining what had taken place and the plan she had agreed to, Amanda felt grateful to be free of the burden of being alone in her knowledge. "That's why I sent Justin and Etzion away. We won't have a choice when we are all together. He will feel it, and he will come for us. He has gone to great lengths to try to stop us from uniting against him. I think it might be the only thing he is afraid of."

"Not even his daughters?"

Amanda shook her head. "Remember, he thinks he has his daughters right where he wants them. The celestial has a lot of tricks up his sleeve, but he is not omnipotent. So, unless we give him a clue that tips him off, he won't come at us until we want him to."

A thoughtful gaze had taken over Emily's features, and she twisted a strand of her curly hair around her finger as she asked, "How can we hope to hold him off long enough to deplete his power?"

Amanda sat up straighter. "You aren't mad about the choice I made?"

Emily answered, "We will do whatever it takes to reach the end, right?"

Kiami nodded, then addressed her in what sounded to Amanda like an unbelieving tone, "Aliens. I only wish that was the craziest thing I ever heard."

A smile blossomed on Amanda's face as she caught Kiami's gaze and spoke. "Good, because it will be up to you to convince the others about the celestials and their origins."

"I don't think convincing them will be a problem, not after the things we have been through," Kiami said, then returned her smile, adding, "I wish I could have seen that wall. It sounded like it was lit up like the night sky."

Amanda admitted, "Now that I think about it, those lights really did remind me of stars and constellations."

Marise offered, "Perhaps they represent the galaxy the celestials came from?"

Amanda shrugged then shifted her attention to him. "I suppose it could have been."

Lines creased his forehead, and he chewed at his lower lip, similar to Emily when she was anxious or worried.

"What is it, Marise?"

"I might be overstepping. I don't have as much experience in matters like this, but to me, it seems fine to say that we will do whatever it takes, but what happens if this form the goddesses mentioned is too big for us to contain? Do we have an actual plan?"

Amanda cocked her head. She had only just made the decision, so she did her best to exude confidence as she answered, "We are going to pool all of our resources."

The lines in his brow creased further, and he brought his hands together on the tabletop. "What do you mean?"

"We are going to ask for help from the few people that might."

"Like who?" Kiami and Emily said in unison as they looked back and forth from her to each other, as if it was the most shocking thing she had said since she began.

Amanda let the smile slide off her face as she stood. She needed them to know she was serious. She placed her hands palm-down on the table and leaned on them. "Anybody that will listen. Beginning with Jacqueline."

27

Kiami - Fight or Flight

The Human Realm

Kiami looked down at the grindyliz. She hadn't asked it to detach from her, yet when she thought of changing form, it had. She assumed that meant the creature didn't want to find out if it could live through the experience.

She reached forward and ran her fingers down its spine as if she were petting Fizzle and listened for changes in the house.

While Amanda had told the tale of her time in the subterranean hold hidden below the garden in the Chaos realm, Kiami sensed the new arrivals, even though the others didn't.

She held her tongue because she knew it was the jinn villagers. She didn't want the story to be put on hold simply because they had returned, and the ones that had entered the house seemed content to listen, so far.

When Amanda explained that Hara Berezaiti had been an actual watch post, just as the area below the garden was, she felt vindicated. Justin had only been one word away from calling her hysterical when she brought the strange debris back with her after the mountain had fallen, and he had made her question her own reasoning. Now it was clear to her that they were remnants of a similar room to the one Amanda had just visited.

The way she described the trio, Amanda made it hard for Kiami to accept that she was linked with them through their very DNA.

She was both elated with the news and caught off guard about retrieving Jacqueline. So much so that she wished Amanda would let Marise go with the boys. She wanted to say more but not with him here; she scarcely knew him.

"If we are successful, we need to be prepared. The things the goddesses said could come to pass." Amanda seemed to be backpedaling.

"*When* we are successful," Kiami interjected.

"Either way, we do have to think about them, even though right now our goal is only to be rid of the celestials."

Kiami believed that the goddesses had been trying to get under her skin. She only had to look at Amanda's regrown arm to understand that she wasn't exaggerating when she said they played games, just like their father.

"How will we decide?" Emily questioned. "It all seems a bit hopeless the way they said it. They told you that if you keep the realms up, there will still be unrest amongst people, and if you let them go, the same is true."

Amanda bowed her head and wrung her hands. "During my time in the Chaos realm, I learned that the people there didn't want war. They just wanted to be free of Abaddon and his master."

"So the inhabitants just want to be free in the way we do?"

"Most of them, yes." She looked back up at Kiami and Emily.

"This is why I worried about the choice I made, but these next decisions we can make together. After we know more about the realms and their inhabitants."

"Meaning they will have to be kept up as long as possible?" Emily asked.

"Yes. The gems were meant to be together, powering the barriers of the world for eons. We should be able to manage to keep them up, if we are careful."

"We will most likely need to use them against the celestial," Emily stated with a wary expression.

"But we will be together. They are weaker the farther apart they get. We have never used them at full power," Amanda said.

"We can't just allow the barrier walls to collapse at once. Too many lives could be lost in the aftermath when they converge," Emily reasoned.

Amanda clasped her hands. "Let's just say we manage to be rid of the celestials without destroying the barriers. Help me find a solution to aim for. Together we can come to the least damaging conclusion."

Kiami knew she was addressing everyone in the room, but she couldn't help but feel that Amanda looked to Emily as if she expected her to take charge and make the decision.

"If they were allowed to merge over time, it would be less of a shock," Emily said as she unwound the strand of hair she had twisted around her finger.

"Agreed."

"Then I think that's what we should aim for after the event," Emily said.

Marise chimed in again. "What if someone else powerful tried to take charge in their absence? Then what?"

Amanda looked up and grimaced at him. "If a new threat arises, we will take care of it. It will be our responsibility, for now at least."

"You will be like a phoenix rising from the ashy fire."

Gemma didn't make herself seen until after Emily hopped up from her chair.

Kiami watched her friend's face as her sudden disbelief dissolved and was replaced by delight.

Emily's eyes twinkled and her mouth twitched as she moved toward her. "You're back."

"Yes, most of us, but it will take time before the town resembles what it did before our departure," she said as she accepted Emily's embrace.

"Where have you been?" Emily questioned, talking into Gemma's shoulder.

"We were close enough to keep an eye on the town and far enough not to interfere."

Emily lifted her head and released Gemma from her grip. "I wish Justin were here. He would be so relieved."

"He will know soon enough."

"We were lost without you."

"Say it enough and you will start believing it. Dry your eyes. You both did fine."

Emily wiped the fresh tears away with her sleeve, then Gemma added, "No more crying until this war is done."

She nodded obediently, then Gemma stepped around her. As she approached the table, she placed a hand on Amanda's shoulder. "That's not an easy choice you made."

"I have had to make hard choices before. At least I feel like this time the choice really was mine," she said matter-of-factly.

"The next fight has only just begun," the jinni responded, then glanced at each of them in turn. "Your anger wages the war, fighting inside of you. Don't let it take over."

28

Emily - They're Here

The Human Realm

When Nina and Cherry appeared, Emily almost jumped out of her skin. Even though it was Nina's home they were in, she hadn't hoped to expect the reunions to continue.

She had missed them all so much after they had abandoned the village, she was having a hard time keeping her word to Gemma not to cry.

She sucked in her breath and hugged Nina, then turned her outstretched arms toward Cherry, who gave her a quick squeeze, then backed out of her embrace. Her familiar ponytail swayed as she reached for her hand.

Emily's heart sank as she spoke. "You should go with Amanda and Kiami to the Emerald Mountains. We can help you get through with the conduit tree in the morning."

"But you only just got here," Emily whined, then shook her hand loose from Cherry's, annoyed.

"There will be plenty of time for celebrations later. And I think you three should stay together until it is necessary to do otherwise," Cherry insisted.

"You talk as if you know the outcome," Amanda said dully.

"Hardly, but we have hope, and we believe in you," Gemma said.

"Touching," Amanda responded, then added, "You could help us with the distraction of the celestial."

"We cannot be at the battlefront. That promise ... the spell, which binds us from speaking of the true history of the world, would also stop us from intervening against the celestial," Gemma said in a hushed tone.

Before Amanda could respond, Nina added, "But we can watch over Marise while you retrieve Jacqueline. It will be fun to get to know him, and, we think, for him to get to know us."

Anxious, Emily chewed lightly at her lip as she questioned whether she was being selfish in her desire to stay. The jinn here had become her surrogate family after she fled her childhood home, and they had been gone for so long.

"The celestials are as good as ticking time bombs," Cherry pleaded.

Nina spoke up. "Now that you have the answers you fought so hard to uncover, how long do you think the sisters will wait while you debate when they could just leave?"

She forced a smile onto her face and gave the jinn a slow, unenthusiastic nod of understanding.

"I will see you again at One Last Bite before you know it," Cherry promised.

Emily pouted as she made her way past the restaurant where Cherry had worked. Although she wasn't hungry, her stomach growled as memories of meals at One Last Bite inundated her thoughts.

Within the days and weeks since the jinn had fled, the windows of the establishment had become covered with a dirty film, and the sign that hung inside the glass that read *Closed* had a spiderweb stretching from one corner as it reached for a part of the door frame she couldn't see from the outside.

She shoved her hand in her pocket and wrapped her fingers around her amethyst for comfort. Amanda had thought they should each carry their gems with them on this journey to aid in their travel, if necessary, but within the time that had passed since she last kept it so close, the stone had come to feel unfamiliar in her clenched fist.

Marise followed behind, and she pointed to the shop Gemma owned. She had been doing her best to try to sound cheery as she showed him around. "I worked there grooming animals until the jinn left."

The sun shone through the window as if it had been freshly cleaned, causing the gold runes decorating the pot sitting on the inner ledge to shimmer slightly.

The yellow and green weed still stood upright within it, although now it had multiple buds growing from its stem.

Emily moved closer to the pane and leaned her forehead against it, as if she would get an answer as to how such a thing could be possible within a building that had been shielded from rain. She knew no one had been inside to tend to the weed since the jinn left.

Emily was reminded of the day she had studied it, admiring the way it had managed to grow up through a crack in the sidewalk and how afterward she had found it was moved by someone into the shop.

She rolled her eyes at herself and backed away from the glass. It was obvious that Gemma had seen her that day and moved the weed, just as she had now replaced the original with a new one.

She spun around and almost walked into Marise. "Sorry."

"What were you looking at?"

"Just something that doesn't belong," Emily huffed as she moved past him and stopped at the sidewalk's edge. She looked down at her shoelaces, one blue and one red. She had always worn them mismatched in this way, at least since she was a child, only now she couldn't recall why.

Marise moved beside her. "Emily?"

She looked up into his eyes; the flecks of bright orange were even more apparent when his hair was left down.

"Yeah, we are here. Well. It's across the street," she said, pulling her eyes from his and turning her head toward the center of town.

She allowed her gaze to hover on the empty bench for a moment before continuing her inspection and bringing it to rest on the carved tree.

The amulets she had helped Justin hang swayed back and forth in the light breeze. Some of them clinked together, reminding her of the musical sound of a wind chime.

"Em?" This time it was Amanda's voice that called to her.

She felt Kiami's hand come to rest on her shoulder. "Are you all right?"

"I am."

She let out a weary sigh, then added, "It's just I was lost when I found this place, but once I did, I felt at home here. Now, I feel lost again."

"You are just anxious. We all are," Kiami said, giving her shoulder a slight squeeze as she did.

"You are probably right," Emily agreed halfheartedly.

"Let's get over to the tree, shall we?" Amanda cooed.

Emily objected, "But Gemma and Cherry aren't even there yet."

The others seemed to ignore her comment, and they began to cross the street.

Emily wrapped her arms around her stomach and followed.

As she reached the first roots that jutted up from the ground near the tree, voices rose all around her, shouting, "Happy birthday!'

Emily's face heated, and a knowing smile spread onto her lips. "It's not my birthday."

Gemma and Cherry were the first to reveal themselves, and within seconds it seemed that every other jinn from town appeared within the borders of the grassy square.

This wasn't the first time they had surprised her by using their ability to remain unseen, and just as the memory surfaced, Mrs. Nazari handed her a cupcake from a tray she carried.

"We just wanted to remind you that you are one of us, Emily. And when this is all over, we will be expecting you to return to your home here within the town."

Emily scolded herself for thinking and acting as if they didn't care, then took the treat and thanked her.

She wouldn't have a lot of time to get reacquainted with her surrogate family, but she would make every second count before she had to leave them.

29

Kiami - Reaching Jacqueline

The Human Realm

To Kiami's relief, with Cherry, Gemma, and Nina's help at the conduit tree, they hadn't needed to use their gems to travel through the barrier of the realms.

The place where they appeared in the Emerald Mountains was more beautiful than she could have imagined.

A single dark tower hovered, its spire looming well above the ground in the far distance as if challenging the mountain range that encircled the valley. The very peaks seemed to shimmer in the sunlight as if they were made of gemstones, like the one she wore on her necklace. Above them, the few white wispy smudges did nothing to dull the brilliant blue of the sky.

Kiami's hair was ruffled in the warm breeze, and she turned in a circle, inspecting the field. Magic seemed to hum and radiate up from the ground as she walked toward a patch of large flower buds, which rose above the knee-high vegetation.

Nearby, she could see several of the bright red flowers had begun to open to allow the sun's rays to kiss their large palm-shaped petals.

Her feet crossed a worn dirt path, and she lifted her eyes to follow it. The trail reached out in one direction toward what appeared to be the remnants of a town. She could see the tops of several worn-looking thatched roofs in the distance.

Amanda reached out and touched her arm, and she spun.

"This area of the fire spirit realm is lovely, isn't it?"

She had been so enamored that she had forgotten she wasn't alone.

Having gained her attention, Amanda removed her hand, and Kiami's eyes flitted over her other friends.

Emily, who hadn't seemed interested in the journey, looked just as pleased at being here as Kiami felt. Her eyes glimmered as she moved toward one of the flowers Kiami had been so taken with only moments ago.

Fizzle had also joined them, and he moved calmly through the field behind her with the very end of his tongue hanging limp from one side of his wide mouth. As he made his way into the deeper grass, his small body almost disappeared from view.

Amanda's words cut through her silent reverie once more, demanding her presence. "I want to show you something."

"Okay." She almost sighed after the word of agreement but stopped herself, and as Amanda moved, she followed.

Back away from the path and closer to the mountains' edge, Amanda lowered herself to kneel in the grass. "That's where they nested, up high in the cracks and crevices."

Amanda pointed towards the curved range. "Aden said they never used to come down from the mountains when he was a youngling. But they must have gotten comfortable in this lower field after most of the jinn left."

Her curiosity piqued, Kiami joined her in front of another patch of flowers just as a red dragon lifted itself from the petals of the one it had been lying on. She watched the small dragons progress as it began lazily flying away, like it didn't have a care in the world.

"I have seen them once before," she whispered back as she watched another, this one as green as the grass below it, uncurl from its resting spot and then stretch out its wings.

"I thought you might want to see them on their home turf," Amanda murmured.

Kiami turned her face toward her and smiled. "Thanks, but I thought we were in a hurry?"

"While I was in the Chaos realm, I realized we have to take these moments as they are available. For us they seem to be in short supply." She didn't miss the sad undertone of Amanda's words, and Kiami's smile faltered.

"Amanda…"

A growl emanated from the grass in front of her, causing Kiami to lose her train of thought as the memory of Fizzle grabbing a dragon out of the air with its tongue resurfaced.

She kept her voice low but firm as she said, "Fizzle. No."

It was too late. The dragon Fizzle had caught sight of took off, and the fuzzy monster was propelling toward the tiny, tasty creature with the end of his frog-like tongue no longer hanging relaxed outside his jaw.

Kiami knew his strike was inevitable when the dragon paused to hover above him and, like the hinge on a door, Fizzle's mouth opened its full width. Then his tongue unfurled from within it, launching toward the thing and wrapping around the creature, squeezing as it curled backward, until it returned to his mouth with his snack sedated.

"Kiami, look up," Amanda warned.

During the commotion, dozens of small, startled dragons had risen from the flowers and darted upward like an angry mob of insects, ready to swarm.

"Their claws and teeth are razor-sharp, Kiami."

She stared up at the mob flapping their leathery wings above her and Fizzle. Some puffed out their chests, and tendrils of smoke rose from their flared nostrils. Others seemed to hover at the ready with their sharp claws poised for attack.

A bright purple one moved forward, stretching its spiked tail out behind it, then circled, moving closer to the ground with each loop.

Soon, the others began to imitate it, following its path.

Fizzle, satisfied with his meal, had begun rolling back and forth in the grass below the angry dragons. Each time he twisted and wriggled, he moved a bit farther away from where she stood.

Kiami knew she could reach the little monster before their attack, but she figured the dragons would have no trouble taking their revenge out on her human form for interfering. So, as she moved forward, she transformed.

To her slight advantage, she was at the top of a naturally raised area in the field, so as she flapped and made her way closer to her friend, she was able to get a little extra lift.

As she passed just above him, she grabbed Fizzle with her talons and hoisted him into the air.

She wanted to carry him high above the angry dragons, but Fizzle, taken by surprise, yelped and then squirmed in her grasp. She beat her wings, flying away from the dragons, then as she swooped back toward them, she ruffled her feathers out and hooted at them in warning.

The creatures stopped their forward trajectory, then turned away from her before disbanding into smaller groups that hastily darted out and away from her.

Satisfied that the dragons had no desire to take her on, she returned to the ground and released her small furry friend.

Fizzle bolted from her sight the moment he was free.

She worried that she had upset the critter but reminded herself that it had been for his own good.

She stretched her wings and shook out her feathers as she prepared to take off once more, meaning to make her way around the entirety of the large field.

When she returned to the ground again, she was surprised to see that although Emily had joined her side, Amanda appeared to have remained in almost the same spot where she had left her, even though she had been in the air for quite some time.

Kiami landed gracefully nearby before returning to her human form, then approached them, speaking casually. "Where do we start to look for Jacqueline?"

"How about up there?" Emily pointed toward the looming tower.

Kiami didn't miss the look of trepidation on Amanda's face at the suggestion. Instead, she offered an alternative route. "How about that way, down the path? It looks like that might be where the jinn residences are or were..."

Amanda's head jerked to the side, and she raised her hands to her hips. "There's really no need for us to venture in either direction," she blurted.

Kiami was taken aback by the remark, and she eyed her wearily, then placed her hands on her hips as if imitating the stance Amanda had just taken before speaking. "And why not?"

"She is coming now. I can see her heading this way." Amanda smirked as she stared ahead. "Long ago, before we officially met, I cast a spell that allows me to see jinn, even when they wish to remain unseen."

She continued, "Jacqueline knows I can see her and you cannot. She is taking her time on purpose, probably in an attempt to get under my skin."

"Why didn't you speak up when Gemma showed up at the house

then?"

Amanda removed her hands from her hips and shrugged. "Why didn't you? I'm pretty sure you could sense their presence in the house as soon as they entered."

Emily turned to Kiami and spoke up. "So you knew the whole town was waiting for me at the square?"

"Apparently not before she could *see* them," Kiami huffed.

"All right, all right," Amanda said, looking back and forth between them. "Does it really matter?"

As Kiami shook her head, Emily responded sheepishly, "Not really."

Amanda lifted her hand and motioned for them to follow. "This is taking too long."

Before they got very far, her guardian must have decided to give up on the ruse, because she allowed herself to be seen.

Kiami's breath caught in her throat at the sight of her. Jacqueline looked as though she always had, and yet now that Kiami knew her guardian was a jinni, to her she seemed like a different person.

Amanda addressed the jinni. "How did you know we were here?"

Jacqueline's eyes twinkled. "For the same reason the dragons got spooked so easily. There are no natural birds of prey that live in this realm, so when I saw Kiami in the air, I knew you had come for me."

Her waist-long brown hair moved with the breeze, and for the first time Kiami noticed how unusual the bright yellow of her eyes truly was.

She knew she should approach to offer her a hug, but her feet seemed unwilling to execute the task.

Under her scrutinizing eyes, the jinni crinkled her nose, then took it upon herself to step forward. "Didn't you miss me, Kiami?"

Kiami gave her a slow nod but remained where she was, at arm's length. Now that they were reunited, she realized she didn't trust the woman as she once had, regardless of the fact that Amanda had been the one to physically take her away.

Her own grief at losing both her guardians had made her forget that in truth, the jinni had changed well before that. Now the painful memories came flooding in.

Kiami took a step back. "I am really happy to see that you are alive, but I don't forgive you."

The jinni's mischievous smirk melted from her lips. "I didn't leave on purpose."

"You were gone long before Amanda banished you. After Rhiannon got sick..." She had said as much before, but in her rush to be reunited, she had forgotten how much Jacqueline's behavior toward her had hurt her.

"I was heartbroken! Then I saw what the moonstone did to that boy on the beach..."

Kiami shook her head and took another step backward. "That was when I needed you most."

30

Amanda - Emerald Mountains

The Jinn Realm

The reunion was not going as expected, and although Amanda didn't want to intervene, she felt she had to say something.

"You could help us now if I remove the spell I cast on you."

Kiami glared at Jacqueline. "Maybe that will fill part of the void you left in my heart."

The jinni cocked her brow. "I'm sure you are aware that I can't join you on the battlefield against the celestial."

Amanda cut in. "But once I release you, you could travel through to other realms and see if anyone would be willing to help."

The jinni raised a hand to her chin and tapped two of her fingers against it. "Who did you have in mind?"

Amanda thought of the note that was still folded in the pocket of her cloak and remembered the words scrawled upon it, the stones that had been left in her tool bag, and how they had been just the right weight to activate the fountains that had led her to the answers she had been seeking all along.

"There is believed to be a faction in the Chaos realm that would like nothing more than to be rid of this overseer. But you would have to be careful not to be found out by the celestial, or it will be for nothing."

"I managed to shield Kiami from him for most of her life. I think I can handle being discreet. My question is, how do you know this faction is in fact real and not just another attempt to lead you all astray?"

Amanda crossed her arms over her chest. "I have seen proof that they exist."

"Okay, I will find them.

"That would be a good start at mending," Kiami murmured in a low voice.

The jinni looked over at her, then back at Amanda. "Who else?" She sounded impatient.

"Well, I think Bloise may help, but it's not safe for jinn where he is..."

"I know the hazards." Her face became taut as she snapped back.

The annoyance in the jinni's voice caused Amanda to tighten her grip on her staff. Even when she had held her captive, she never saw her get so frustrated.

Jacqueline threw a fleeting glance in Kiami's direction as if looking for approval then added, "I will volunteer to go inform the wizard Bloise as well."

"Traveling to him would be much more dangerous for you," Emily noted.

"I am aware of the hatred the people around him have for my kind. If found out, they would look at me in the same way she is now." Jacqueline nodded in her estranged ward's direction. "Perhaps by my taking on this risky task, she will be able to find it within herself to forgive me."

Kiami shifted her stance and looked down at her feet.

Jacqueline's face went slack for a moment, then her forehead wrinkled as she spoke again. "I won't lie and say that I don't hold any ill will toward you, Amanda. But in regard to aiding you in this matter, I will do what is within my power."

Amanda nodded. She had expected the jinni to hold some animosity toward her, and she still wasn't entirely convinced by her cordial display.

Emily stepped forward as if she was wary of the jinni as well and was readying herself to intervene then asked, "How do we remove the curse?"

Amanda lifted her staff into the air, then brought the end straight back down, pressing the tip into the ground and keeping it upright at her side.

The movement caused the mud still encasing her gem to crumble from around it, once again revealing the black diamond she had covered.

Then she reached into her pocket and pulled out the small folding knife she had brought along. "We remove it in much the same way I cast it."

She handed it to Jacqueline, then produced a folded square from her other pocket. As she unfolded the page to reveal the rune she had drawn on it, she looked at the jinni expectantly.

Jacqueline popped the blade out and then pressed the tip into the palm of her opposite hand until blood began to pool from the new wound.

As she dropped the knife at her feet, Amanda pressed the rune over her bleeding cut and whispered the necessary words.

When she pulled the page back away, it burst into flames as if it had been soaked in lighter fluid rather than blood.

She released the sheet and let it burn to ash as it made its way to the ground, then bent down to retrieve the knife.

When she grasped it, the jinni asked, "Where are you planning for the event to take place?"

"Hara Berezaiti," Amanda responded as she wiped the knife on the ground before closing it and straightening herself.

"To the watch post of the stars, it is then," the jinni said.

"It's not exactly as it was anymore. The mountain has fallen."

Jacqueline looked at her with pity in her eyes, and Amanda couldn't help but feel she knew her secret: that she had collapsed the mountain, sacrificing those within it.

"It's no matter to me. I'm sure you did what you had to do," Jacqueline added in a mocking tone.

"I think that's enough." Amanda shoved the closed knife into her pocket and placed one hand on her hip.

"Fine, then. I should be on my way if I mean to make it to the Chaos realm, then to Bloise in time, anyway. And I will, Kiami. That I promise."

The jinni took another step toward her, but her charge recoiled as if burdened by the idea of a real farewell.

The sight pained Amanda, not because she cared that their relationship was mended, but because she didn't like to see Kiami in pain.

The jinni didn't make another attempt at speaking with Kiami but instead made herself unseen to her before moving wordlessly away to set off on her mission.

When Jacqueline was no longer visible to her, Amanda turned to Kiami. It looked like the blood had drained from her face. "Are you ready to return to the human realm? This trip won't be as easy."

She nodded.

"Em, are you ready?"

"I think so."

"Grab your gems in one hand and place the other on my shoulders." When she felt the hands grasp her, she reached out for her staff and called to her shadow magic.

31

Kiami - Battle Call

The Human Realm

The effects of traveling with the help of the shadow magic had not had a chance to wear off, and Kiami's stomach twisted, unable to settle.

She attempted to ignore the sensation; she wanted to stay busy. If she rested, as Amanda suggested, she would think of things she had no desire to focus her attention on, like the way she had let Jacqueline leave without uttering a goodbye.

She didn't want to harbor anger for Jacqueline, but she couldn't keep the feeling at bay no matter how hard she tried.

Emily also seemed uninterested in taking a break and had agreed with her when she urged them on.

Instead of the jinn town, when they had arrived back in the human realm, they found that Amanda had brought them to a densely wooded area, and it was one Kiami was unfamiliar with.

Here the smell of pine surrounded her as they made their way through heavy brush until they found evidence of a trail, almost covered in leaves and needles, as if it hadn't been maintained in some time.

Amanda lifted her staff, muttering, then a thick, inky black shadow began to stretch outward from the gem at the top, twisting and snaking forward like the syrup of a maple tree cutting a path down its trunk.

Kiami followed wordlessly behind as Amanda went where the tendril of her magic led, regardless of the trail's shape, and she became unsteady at the sudden upcropping of roots on more than one occasion.

After some time, she found herself being guided off the trail and marching toward a tree that seemed stunted and twisted in ways the surrounding forestry did not. When she stood nearby, she discovered that it was barely her height, and the knuckle-filled branches seemed devoid of life.

Amanda lowered herself to its base and cleared the woodland debris away with her hand. The action revealed that the tree held carved runes that looked very similar to the ones that encircled the tree in the jinn village.

"Why are we here?" Kiami asked, growing impatient.

"This is where my staff was made. And up there," Amanda swiveled herself to point toward the small hill behind her, "is where I found Erol. It is the place that this all began, for me, anyway."

Emily sat down by Amanda. "Do you mean to look for evidence that this is another watch post?"

"Not exactly, although I do plan on making a trek up the hill. First, I thought you could use help in funneling your magic."

"With a staff like yours?"

"Well, we will have to see what the tree gives us."

Amanda pulled the folding knife from her pocket, and Kiami could see that its handle held several small rubies as well as some writing. She hadn't noticed the tiny details before.

Although she had been watching Amanda's actions as she lifted the spell, she had felt a million miles away.

Amanda passed the knife to Emily, giving her clear instructions as she did. "Dig a hole beneath the tree, near a root, and bury this within it. Then bring me what the tree gives you."

Emily unfolded the knife as Amanda stood back up and joined Kiami at her side.

"Where are you going?"

"We will be just over here, a bit farther away. This part is for you to do alone."

Amanda wrapped her arm around Kiami's shoulder and moved with her back toward the trail.

"I would like you to stay with us here longer, but if you want to go, I won't try to stop you."

Kiami wrung her hands. "It's not that I don't want to be here, exactly."

"There is no need to explain. The more I learn about my own parents, the less I wish I knew. So I understand how you could feel betrayed. But it has been my experience that the more you fight thoughts and emotions, the stronger and more stuck you will become."

Kiami pushed to press on with her task. "Right now, I just need to keep moving forward."

"All right. Just promise me you will be careful."

"I promise."

Her heart thundered in her ears as she turned away from Amanda to take her leave.

She took a few steps and then wiped her sweaty palms against the fabric of her dress before turning her face back to see Amanda had not budged. "I will do my best to heed your advice regarding Jacqueline."

32

Emily - Gifts

The Human Realm

Emily's disappointment that they hadn't returned to the jinn village right away had dissolved once she had learned the purpose of their visit to the forest.

The idea of having her own staff to help focus her magic intrigued her.

After she finished the task Amanda had given her, Emily sat back on her heels and looked up at the canopy. The other trees loomed over her in a way that she found both menacing and majestic. Above her, small amounts of light trickled in between the full branches, keeping the area alive with shadows, yet the rays that did cut through sparkled and gleamed like a well-polished knife, cutting down to the ground.

A snapping from above her caused her to refocus her attention on the gnarled tree she sat beneath.

Shivers ran up her spine as she watched a short limb that had broken free make its way down beside her with a thud.

When she saw where it landed, she understood the sudden chill she felt. In the milliseconds that had passed, the area around her and the tree had changed considerably.

The ground where she sat now appeared to be covered in a layer of frost. She pushed herself to her feet to escape the cold ground and was brought face to face with rows of pink and white flowers that had sprouted along the short tree's branches.

Emily bent down to retrieve the fallen gift, just as Amanda reappeared from behind a tree.

"Nice."

The limb was only about a foot long and about as thick as her clenched fist at one end, while the other tapered off into a thin point. Emily looked from her gift to the staff that Amanda held. "It's so small."

Amanda cocked an eyebrow. "I think it's perfect."

Unconvinced, Emily lifted one brow back at her as she tested its weight in her hand. "It's pretty light too."

Seeming as if she chose to ignore the observation, Amanda continued her instructions. "Get your amethyst out and hold it to the thicker end."

Emily drew the gem from her pocket and pressed the flattest side to the limb as instructed. "Like this?"

"Yes, but don't call to your magic, just keep it steady," Amanda warned.

Amanda moved closer and reached out to place her own hand on top of Emily's, then muttered something in a language Emily couldn't understand.

She tried to open her fingers as she felt the sensation of movement below them, but Amanda's own hand bore down on it harder, stopping her from letting go.

She again muttered the foreign words unintelligible to Emily's ears, then loosened her hold as something began to sprout from the edge of

Emily's palm.

Amanda slid her own hand down the length of the evolving limb, and Emily wiggled her fingers above the new growth, careful not to let go.

"It's done," Amanda assured her, releasing her hold.

When Emily shifted the weapon in her hand, she saw that the new growth had twisted around the end of the limb and the gem, securing them together in place. Then, while she ran her fingers over the transformed branch, the rough outermost layer of the visible area began to flake away at her touch.

Soon, the dark brown coloring of the surface was gone, and a lower layer of marbled browns and yellows canvased the now smoother exterior.

With the exception of the pointed end, which appeared to be sharp enough to break skin given the right force, the results reminded her of a human children's toy. That, along with the thought of carrying the new weapon around in her hand all the time, caused her to look at it with skepticism.

Emily chewed at her lip, concentrating on concealing the disappointment from her face. She stuck the wand between two fingers and twirled it like a baton as she thought about where she could get a holster of some sort.

"You don't like it."

"I will get used to it," Emily said matter-of-factly. "Where's Kiami?"

"Since seeing Jacqueline wasn't as satisfying as she had hoped it would be, she set off to inform the others."

Considering she had witnessed the strained reunion firsthand, Emily couldn't say she was surprised by the news.

"Do you want to go up the hill with me?"

"Might as well; you brought me along for the ride."

Her answer was met with a wide but rather short-lived smile.

As they attempted to climb the small hill, Emily found herself grasping for outstretched branches with her free hand again and again.

She marveled at how the task of carrying the small tool could make her feel so unsteady on her feet. Although she didn't voice her complaint, Amanda stopped suddenly and yanked a wisteria vine from one of the trees along their route.

She made a quick turn toward Emily and handed it to her. "Tie it around your waist, like this." Then she pointed to her belt. "If you slip the end through, your new weapon should stay snug enough."

Emily accepted the vine and tied it around herself, then plucked the few leaves off before slipping the end of her wand through the loop. "Thanks."

"You can thank me when the celestials are gone," Amanda said and then spun on her heels to finish the ascent.

At the top, a bold yellow sign announced that the area was posted. The smaller words below that read *Keep Out*. A single raised row of linked chains encircled the area of the ground that they had neglected to fill back in after it was excavated.

Amanda bent down and picked several brightly colored flowers.

To Emily, their buds looked to be only a few shades darker than the green stem that held it upright, but the bracts themselves were so flamboyant that they made them look like a fine-tipped artist's tool. She watched in silent wonder as Amanda ceremoniously tossed them over the side without offering any word of explanation.

Contemplating what it meant, Emily reached up and twisted one of her curls around her finger. "Are we looking for anything in particular?"

Amanda began to make her way around the feeble barrier before she responded, "There used to be five pillars here."

She pointed and made a circle as if she was referring to the entire hilltop. "They were maybe seven or eight feet tall... I remember wondering if it had been part of the foundation of a small building."

Emily glanced around the outer perimeter but saw no sign of the pillars. "Perhaps they were removed by the excavation team?"

"There was a collapse involving them, and I was pulled into a stone cellar of some sort."

She peered over the chain where she had flung the flowers, and Emily followed suit. Although she couldn't make out what lay at the bottom of the dugout pit, to her the hole seemed to hold only natural debris that you would expect to see in the woods.

The visible sides consisted of dark, rich dirt with a few roots and branches that poked out here and there at random angles.

Emily unwound her curl from her finger and straightened up. She believed Amanda had been in a cellar, as she said, but she saw no evidence of the stone walls.

When she looked back up at her friend, she saw Amanda shudder visibly. "Even though I couldn't see down there, I know there was more to it than this."

"Someone could have used a machine to clear it out," Emily offered, still wondering in the back of her mind about the flowers.

"Or magic," Amanda countered. "Or technology we don't know about."

"True. But why bother?"

"To keep us from learning the truth too soon, I suppose."

"Or maybe when you fell you were transported. You said all the trees connected the realms."

Amanda looked at her thoughtfully then nodded in her direction. "I couldn't bring myself to come up here when I returned before, and I think I just wanted to be sure."

"This is where you found Erol's prison?"

"Yes."

"So, you really just wanted to come up here to gain closure? To say goodbye?"

Amanda shrugged.

Emily furrowed her brow as she wondered if the simple act of tossing flowers down the hole had really helped her. "Did you accomplish what you came for?"

"Yes." Amanda spun around and reached for Emily's hand. "I did. Now let's go collect Marise. Cherry promised to have a meal waiting for you at One Last Bite. I'm sure you are eager to get to it."

Emily responded with a quick nod before posing another question. "In the morning, we are going to Hara Berezaiti to await the others?"

"That's the plan. The longer we procrastinate, the higher our chances of the celestial learning what we are up to. We aim to catch him off guard, not the other way around."

Emily was in no hurry to get to battle, but deep down she knew Amanda spoke the truth. As she accepted her hand, she placed the other on the hilt of her wand.

When she grasped the gem, she was relieved to find that the action seemed to give her comfort once more.

A smile emerged on her face, and as they made their way back down the hill, she allowed herself to think about how proud her jinn family would be when she helped to rid them of the celestials once and for all.

33

Kiami - Anger and Indifference

The Human Realm

Kiami hadn't wasted any time flying to the coordinates Amanda had given her. The journey by flight had only taken a few hours.

When she arrived in the small hamlet where Etzion lived, she perched across the way from his home upon one of the many willow trees that lined the edge of the street, intent on making sure the location was safe before approaching the pair.

The stone cottage that his family lived in was quaint and looked to her like something straight from a fairy tale with its ornate pink trim, pale blue shutters, and steep, sloping roof. The natural wood shingles overlapped on the way down, creating a wave-like pattern, which worked to intensify the impression.

Although there were equally small homes that flanked the left and right, the house seemed secluded due to the vegetation that ran wild between it and the neighboring abodes.

Kiami had known he had a large family, consisting of his guardians and multiple half-brothers and sisters, but it seemed to her every time a pair of the siblings left the house, three more entered the small cottage. Despite her assertion that she needed to keep busy, she found herself somewhat contented by the sight, and the longer she watched, the less she wanted to interfere.

Being a single child, she supposed her curiosity about the inner workings of such a family was only natural. She was surprised to see that crowded as they must have been inside, from the outside his family unit seemed to be in harmony. Not a soul appeared from behind the closed door that didn't have a smile on their face, even Justin, who seemed to have been welcomed into the fold with open arms.

Kiami had watched him join a game in which he, Etzion, and a few others took turns balancing, then bouncing a small object off their elevated feet. Given the ease of his interactions with them, she couldn't help but think he could easily have been mistaken for another member of the family if she hadn't known better.

She had observed, fascinated, for some time even after the game had ended, unable to bring herself to leave the tree before Blaine showed up in wisp form. The arrival broke her steady concentration and allowed thoughts of Jacqueline to invade once again.

Reluctantly, Kiami had given in and followed the bluish balls of wispy smoke down to the ground, where she would be at least partially concealed by overgrown shrubbery before transforming out of her owl form.

She couldn't help but notice how as the wisps Blaine moved with such ease, and she wondered if he should have been the one to deliver the warning to those in the Chaos realm, and Bloise, for that matter.

Her cheeks reddened at the idea, and she crossed her arms over her stomach. She knew that her anger had been the reason why Jacqueline had volunteered.

She eyed Blaine's form warily. Even though his movements were swift, it took him much longer to take on a human shape than her. She watched in silence while the foggy-looking balls of energy merged and a human-esque silhouette formed, then lost its transparency.

After it solidified, she closed her eyes and took a deep breath.

A breeze blew past her, cooling her cheeks and pushing her long, loose hair away from her face. When she opened her eyes again, she dropped her arms back at her sides in indifference; she was still mad at her guardian, but she was a little worried too.

When she looked up, strange eyes stared into hers. Bright yellow flecks seemed to burst through the irises, which swirled with a smoke gray haze.

The corners of Blaine's mouth lifted into a smile, then the being nodded in her direction and offered a greeting.

"Hello, Kiami."

The last time Blaine had morphed into human form to talk to her, the facial characteristics had remained blurred, giving only an impression of where a nose, mouth, and eyes belonged. In fact, the ocular sockets had appeared empty. This time the features were more pronounced, yet apart from those startling eyes, they still seemed subtle.

"Hi, Blaine. You look different."

"Yes well, when last we spoke, I was literally in two places at once. At this moment, however, you have my undivided attention."

I wish I could say the same for myself, Kiami thought as she shifted on her feet.

The being spoke again. "I could make my skin more apparent and add hair to my physique if it makes you more comfortable. But then I would need to get some clothes..."

Her eyes found Blaine's again, and she flashed a sheepish smile. "No. I think you look amazing. I just have a few things on my mind."

"Is that why you were watching them?"

Kiami lifted one shoulder in a small shrug. "I guess. How long have you been here?" She raised her hands to her cheeks as they began to feel warm again.

Being the first time they had been face to face since she learned the true nature of the wisps, the idea that Blaine could be spying undetected at any time sank in, making her feel uneasy and a little embarrassed.

"Not long." Blaine let out an audible sigh. "I do know what it's like to have my mind on more than one thing at a time. And often, keeping watch over a situation is all that's within my ability, so that's why I inquired."

Kiami uncovered her cheeks, then pulled her eyes away and trained them on the house across the road before she breathed out the words, "How do you manage to stay focused when you can be in more than one place at once?"

"Practice, I suppose. Sometimes it's more difficult than others, and the more thinly I spread myself, the less I can physically do."

Digging for information or a new distraction, she asked, "Can you describe it to me?"

Blaine's head tilted to the side. "I'm not sure I know what you mean."

"Where were you before you came here to find me staring?"

"Ah, well, that requires a multifaceted response."

"Meaning you were in more than one place?"

"Yes. Think of me as a tree, and the farther I spread my branches, the thinner they become."

"Kind of like the gems? Amanda said they are stronger together. The farther they are from each other, the weaker they become."

Blaine's head moved from side to side as if looking for something or someone before the being's attention snapped back to her. "The day is almost done, so I have seen quite a bit."

"Please. I am not ready to confront the others with Amanda's plan yet."

"I have learned the hard way that too much interference on my part can cause more harm than good. Still, I suppose it wouldn't cause any adverse effects if I told you that before coming here most of me was either in the jinn village watching Marise or following Amanda up the hill to the place where she first found the artifact that held Erol captive. Emily was with her, of course, and sporting a wand of sorts with her gem fastened to the top. I did not make myself known to anyone. I was simply observing at that point because I had also sent a few wisps on another errand after I caught wind of why you had gone to the Emerald Mountains."

Kiami held her breath as she waited for Blaine to elaborate. When her chest began to burn with the need for release, she pushed it out forcefully and sucked in fresh air. Her voice sounded raspy and harsh as she addressed the storyteller. "That's all you're going to tell me?"

"There isn't much more to say. I didn't go to the girls until you had already left them, and their trek was quite uneventful, as far as I could tell. They were preparing to return to the village when I decided that I should make my way here and find you. I wanted to verify that you had arrived, with the intention of joining you so I could properly introduce myself to Justin and Etzion."

Questions pushed their way out of her mouth. "Well, where were you before that? We sent Jacqueline to recruit sympathizers. Can you tell me if she made it?"

"Is Jacqueline what's really troubling you?"

She shrugged. "Partially, I guess."

"I can't say for sure if she made it to her destinations, but the errand I mentioned was for reconnaissance at the palace where Bloise lives. I can only tell you this: the old wizard was not there."

Kiami could hear a hint of desperation in her own voice as she asked, "Do you think she made it then?"

"We shouldn't speculate."

Given the warning Blaine had made about interferences causing harm, she figured she had been pushing her luck with the questions, so she wasn't surprised by the response as she conceded, "Fine."

She shuffled her feet again as she thought over what was said, then smirked; whether Blaine knew it or not, the small amount of information they had offered about Bloise's absence made her feel better. She crossed her arms in front of her and poised a new question: "How was Marise getting along in the village?"

"Kiami, it really is getting late, and it seems like you have had quite a long day."

34

Kiami - Interference

The Human Realm

If Blaine had neglected to point it out to her twice, Kiami wouldn't have realized that the day was nearing its end. When her eyes drifted to the horizon, the sun's red velvet silhouette almost appeared heart-shaped as it sank, while an equally brilliant arrow of light protruded from each side. To her it looked as if it had been shot through in an attempt to force it into submission.

She kept her eyes trained on the spot as she spoke again, urging the half-blood to tell her more. "Please, Blaine."

"I suppose, if it helps you. I just... I need a minute to think before I continue."

She gave a low groan. "I'll just be waiting, admiring the sunset, until you're ready."

"Kiami, are you sure you want to hear my worries?"

She turned back to face Blaine and placed her hands on her hips. "Don't try to talk your way out of it. You already agreed."

Blaine took a noncombative stance, with hands raised to chest height, then stepped backward and lowered them again before hunkering down in the grass. "To properly answer your question, I would have to go to earlier in the day. Right after you, Amanda, and Emily left for the Emerald Mountains... But I suppose it would be best that someone besides the jinn knows, and I fear it couldn't be Amanda or Justin. They are too hot-headed. I wouldn't want either to jump to conclusions in this matter."

Kiami raised a questioning eyebrow, then knelt down to join Blaine. "What has happened now?"

"That's the thing. I am not sure. It can be hard to keep dibs on everyone. Some of us seem to attract more negative attention than the rest."

Kiami couldn't help but feel that Blaine was placing blame, even if the being didn't realize it. "You mean Amanda?"

"The celestial did seem to be concentrating his efforts on her, at least until more of our paths started intersecting."

Kiami interrupted, "Weren't you helping to promote that?"

Blaine seemed to allow the question to bounce off. "The point is, for a time I kind of lost track of Marise. There was so much going on, especially around when Amanda sent you to spy on Emily. Do you remember that?"

Kiami began to pick at the grass that surrounded her, feeling the slender blades, then slowly pulled them out of the dirt one at a time as she thought of the car accident she had inadvertently caused when she arrived to observe Emily. "I remember."

She looked up from her small mound of clippings and added, "I thought we were talking about today?"

"We are. But this is important for context."

"So, what you are saying is that while the four of us were distracting you..."

"That's not what I meant. Marise seemed well cared for, so when I went to eavesdrop and found he had abandoned his family, I was concerned. And when I finally found him again, he seemed different."

"That's ominous."

"Sorry. I just meant after I tracked him down, he was always looking over his shoulder like he was watching, waiting for someone to come for him. The change made me assume there was a good reason he left his home. I tried to help him as best I could without drawing attention to myself."

"So, he was scared? Do you think he had an encounter with the celestial or one of his minions?"

"From your own experiences, you know that the celestial will stop at nothing to watch this planet and its inhabitants come to a horrific end due to this ongoing feud with his daughters."

The reminder of what they were trying to stop caused a fresh crop of goosebumps to rise along her arms, and Kiami crossed them in front of herself as Blaine continued. "But in truth, I was never sure of what happened."

The words that slipped from her mouth sounded harsher than she meant. "If you were that concerned, why didn't you transform and ask?"

"I needed to keep a low profile, remember. It was the only way I managed to stay out of the celestial's crosshairs."

She found it was hard to gauge Blaine's underlying feelings, and more than a little irritated by the admittance, she prodded more. "So, you were only looking out for yourself?"

"Kiami, maybe this was a bad idea. You still don't seem quite like yourself."

She had realized the question would sting before she let it escape her mouth, but she didn't care for the way Blaine seemed most concerned with the well-being of Blaine above all else.

The being's voice never wavered. "Kiami, I have used my ability to help all of you. If I had been removed from the equation, you wouldn't have half the answers you have now."

The blood drained from her face as she questioned her own actions, wondering if she had been looking for an argument all along. "Sorry. I didn't mean to make insinuations."

"It's okay. I know I speak a bit too plainly sometimes. I will try to be more cognizant of my word choice. Shall I continue?"

Kiami nodded as she steered the conversation back to Marise. "At any rate, whatever the catalyst was, we know that he doesn't mean ill will toward the jinn, since he followed Amanda through their barrier without any adverse effects."

"Correct. I also don't want him to feel like we don't trust him, because then he may be less inclined to place trust in us. I would have tried to dig deeper to understand, but as you know time is no longer on my side."

The goddesses had made it clear that they would be willing to let their father destroy the planet if she and the other half-bloods failed. Amanda had said as much. Their only hope, if they were to have any chance at draining the celestial's powers, was not only to have all seven gems at the battle, but also the half-bloods that could wield and extrapolate their own abilities with them. Kiami nodded to show that she understood the point. "We need to be unified for the plan to work."

Blaine pointed a finger in her direction. "You, Kiami, gave me the answer I needed."

"How's that?"

"When the three of you headed to the Emerald Mountains, I brought myself together to bring up my concerns with the jinni. Of course, they answered in riddles, pointing out in a roundabout way that Marise was probably less a threat himself and rather how it was more likely that his family had been threatened."

"And so...."

"Well, they changed the subject, of course."

Kiami smirked. "I bet they did."

"Through the jinni, I learned that the grindyliz are pretty intuitive, and although they can't control you, they will use their own thoughts and knowledge to help persuade the actions of their symbiotic companion, if they think it's in the best interest of both of them."

"I see. So, you insinuated to the creature that if he could keep Marise's mind off his family, whom you assume was threatened, he would make a good companion."

"Pretty much. At least until such time when the creature can be returned to its own realm."

"And later, Marise just agreed?"

"The young man still feels a bit like an outsider. Less so with his new companion."

The use of the grindyliz to stop Marise from thinking about his family felt wrong to Kiami, but she could come up with no alternative solution. "We will make an effort to get the creature back to its realm, right?"

"Yes."

Kiami stood up and made a show of dusting herself off. "We better go brief Justin and Etzion."

35

Amanda - Saying Goodbye

The Human Realm

It wasn't until Amanda and Emily had descended the hill and returned to the jinn village that she pondered whether she should have had Emily practice using the wand before they left the forest.

When they returned, they discovered that Gemma and Cherry had taken it upon themselves to give Marise some pointers regarding his skills. The pair seemed confident in his abilities to handle himself but were eager to mention that they had not involved the use of his gem in this training.

It was this reminder that made her decide in the end that such practices wouldn't be worth the risk to the barriers. It also caused her to second-guess her own actions in the forest.

The wand's creation had seemed like a good idea, but she now had to admit to herself that it was both a dangerous exercise and little more than an excuse to return to the site all along.

Even the use of her gem on the trail now seemed selfish, but given that neither Emily nor Kiami had called her out on it, she knew the pair were probably distracted by their own thoughts and inner turmoil about the fight ahead, just as she was.

In fact, she was quite sure that at least part of the emotions Kiami was experiencing toward her guardian had more to do with anxiety about the coming battle and less to do with her perceived abandonment by Jacqueline than Kiami would be willing to admit.

Prefight jitters were not uncommon and understandable given that most of the battles fought in the past had been in the spur of the moment, defensive fights. She had not had time to think about them beforehand. This one was different in that she knew it was coming, and at least for now she was in control of how it would come about.

Now aware that her own self-doubts had been keeping her from organizing her thoughts in the best way, she understood that this was her true reason for returning to the site.

She knew that she needed to quell her building anxiety by refocusing her attention, and the task she had chosen was saying goodbye.

At the time, she hadn't realized she was seeking something to help her on the battlefield in any moment that might arise where she needed to be snapped back from wandering thoughts brought on by her own mind's fight-or-flight response.

Earlier, when she had noticed the orange and red castilleja, Amanda had known they would be the perfect symbol for what she had lost and what she was fighting to save. As she plucked them, she fondly remembered how she had spotted one of the prairie flowers during her first trip here with her father. Before everything changed.

She smiled sheepishly as she thought about how he had corrected her when she referred to the plant by its more common nickname, often used due to its slender paintbrush-like appearance.

Later, when she had thrown them down into what remained of her first underground prison, she had even whispered a goodbye to her father, Erol, Aden, and her mother.

The act, simple as it was, had made her feel better in a way she couldn't quite pinpoint, and as she watched Emily's spirit lift the moment she was reunited with her adoptive clan, she realized they would be able to help Emily in the same way if doubts began to take hold.

36

Emily - Fallen Mountain

The Human Realm

Even though she had known her time there would be short, back at the jinn village Emily had found it easy to relax in the company of her surrogate family. After she had enjoyed her meal, she somehow managed to find peaceful sleep that lasted through the night.

However, when she awoke to dawn's light breaking across the sky, her stomach knotted with dread as her mind filled with vivid scenarios in which none of them survived the onslaught of the angered being.

Try as she might to push them away and replace them with good memories, she couldn't seem to make her brain cooperate.

She became so engrossed in them that the sudden rapping at her door caused her to jump from the bed and reach for her wand. She brought it to her chest as she approached the entrance, whispering, "Who is it?"

Amanda's voice seemed to echo in from beyond the door as she answered, "It's me."

Emily took in a deep breath. Her face felt hot, and her cheeks were damp. She dropped her arms but kept the weapon wrapped tightly between her fingers as she pulled the door open a few inches to peek out. "Is Marise with you? "

She didn't want the newcomer to see her so distraught.

"No."

Emily pulled the door open and ushered Amanda into the room, then closed it again. "Is it time to go already?"

Amanda nodded but moved to sit at the end of her bed then patted the spot next to her.

Emily stared at the spot for a moment, dazed, then moved to take a seat beside her.

"It's okay to be scared, Em. You have prefight jitters, that's all."

"Everything is about to change."

"I know. But it's not the first time we have had to deal with such a change."

"What if we lose and the celestials continue their feud, destroying everything? There is so much more than our lives at stake."

"What if we don't?" Amanda countered. "You just need something to focus on when your mind starts to wander."

"I have attempted to keep the thoughts at bay."

"Let me guess, you keep trying to bring up good memories, but your mind wanders, always returning to that dark place?"

Emily grazed her lip with her teeth, afraid that if she agreed out loud, it would somehow make the thoughts worse.

Amanda gave her a knowing smile. "There's too much for you to grasp on to. You need to find and focus on just one small thing."

Emily thought of the brightly colored offering she had seen Amanda throw into the pit. "Were the flowers your one thing?"

"Yes, but they remind me of many things, including what I am fighting for and against. In that way it helps."

Emily squeezed her eyes shut. And as she thought about what she was fighting for, a clear image of Gemma came into focus.

She released the grip on her wand, dropping it beside her, then wiped the tears from her cheeks.

"Better?"

She nodded.

"Then let's get Marise and go to the site."

"Are we going to use your shadow magic to make the trip?"

"No, the jinn have offered to help us with the journey. Have you traveled with them before?"

Emily shook her head.

"It's like walking with the wind. You will feel a breeze swirling all around you, then it will lift you and carry you, as if you were part of it."

As Emily released the hand of the villager who had helped her make her way to the mountain, the air all around seemed to cease movement, and before she could thank the three volunteers, they had made themselves unseen.

She hadn't known the travel companions well, but she was glad for the company and grateful that she hadn't had to make the journey using Amanda's shadow magic, not just because it imposed risk to the barriers, but also because she always felt a bit off in her gut afterword.

She moved her eyes over Amanda, noting that her own gaze had risen skyward.

Figuring she was watching the jinn's hasty departure, Emily surveyed the land around them instead.

Emily could still see the devastation of the fallen mountain, even though she had never visited the site before it was reduced to ruin. The evidence remained in the land that was left behind in the wake and still persisted to be conspicuously bare, even in the weeks since it had happened.

She could only guess that when the mountain crumbled, it caused the land to shift down, tearing vegetation and trees from the ground, roots and all. She could see trails of the ashy gray remains of dried-out trunks and branches all around the outer perimeter.

The ground under her felt solid but held deep cracks as if deprived of water since the event. She thought of the river that Kiami and Amanda had mentioned, and she presumed the landslide could have buried or blocked part of it, altering its original course.

She supposed this was a good place to fight. Less to destroy, since it had already been dealt a savage blow it would probably never recover from.

She thought of Gemma as the fluttering sensation returned to her stomach. When her nerves settled once more, she looked back over at Amanda, thankful for her advice earlier in the day and a bit envious of her ability to conceal her fears.

To her, Amanda appeared ready to strike at any moment. Her face was hard and blank as she seemed to examine every centimeter of the area in preparation for the battle ahead.

The plan was to set up a base camp along the edge of the site, where they could rest. It was Emily's job to find a spot partially obscured from view that could be used for such a purpose.

She glanced over at Marise, wondering if she should invite him to join her as she searched the outer perimeter.

Although he had seemed accepting of his fate from the beginning, he now smiled in a way that Emily believed conveyed he had no idea what he was in for, but then again, he was now accompanied by the displaced grindyliz.

Emily wondered at the pairing, which Gemma and Cherry had arranged during their time with him.

From what she had seen of her friend when she had helped the creature, she hadn't liked the way the critter seemed to affect Kiami's response time. Or the idea that it could possibly affect her thoughts, but the decision had been made and Amanda had seemed okay with it.

Perhaps, she thought, Gemma and Cherry felt the creature help to keep Marise balanced and contented. But she doubted the animal would fare much better with him than it would have with Kiami, although it was true that he didn't change form when he used his magic as her shape-shifting friend did.

Emily turned away from him and began her search.

37

Kiami - Battle Cry

The Human Realm

The cave Emily had found along the bordering area where the mountain had once stood reminded Kiami of Etzion's house, not in outer appearance but in its size compared with the number of people that were expected to be inside.

All together now, the seven were cramped in the bean-shaped remains of what had most likely been a much larger cavity with interconnecting caverns before the destruction of the summit had caused parts of it to shift and crumble.

She supposed the interior wouldn't matter in the end, since they didn't expect to be at their base location for an extended amount of time, given the celestial's desire to be in control.

Kiami lowered herself onto a natural stone shelf that happened to be at just the right height to serve as a chair. Despite the fact that there were several such outcroppings within the small room, she and Amanda were the only two in their party to make use of them in such a way, most likely due to the uneven walls that if leaned against threatened discomfort.

She looked from Blaine to Etzion, then Justin. They had all taken her explanation of what Amanda had found in the Chaos realm pretty well, considering; in fact, she had been a bit surprised that Justin didn't attempt to argue about the plan to draw the celestial to them at Hara Berezaiti.

Now, she peered over at her other young accomplices. Emily fidgeted with her hair, and Marise stared off at the opposite wall from where he sat, as if in deep concentration. Amanda had only just rejoined them.

It seemed they had arrived earlier than she anticipated, and she had made a hasty retreat to parts unknown as the rest of them stocked the cave with their meager supplies.

During her leave, Kiami had scolded herself for agreeing to use Etzion's stone to travel. She had assumed there was no point in laying low any longer, so she hadn't thought too much about it until she saw the look of distress on Amanda's face and the way she had left them without much of an explanation.

At any rate, she thought, it was too late to take it back, and whatever repercussions were caused by the stone's use must have been minimal or were simply too far away for them to catch sight of.

For now, at least, everything was as quiet around them as it could be, considering that the current characteristics of the cave's natural shape and size seemed to amplify every sound, whether it was someone brushing loose debris out from under them or talking in a whisper.

Amanda stood suddenly and spun in a circle. "I started out with a clear idea of what I wanted to say, and now that the time has come, I am at a loss."

Emily pushed herself up and stood at Amanda's side, wringing her hands in front of her. "I think Amanda has forgotten that the fewest words in their rawest form can have the greatest impact. But it is something she has reminded me of on more than one occasion, so while she is at a loss for them, I will do my best to fill her shoes."

Justin and Etzion clapped and cheered at her announcement. When their voices died down, she went on, "Our time has come. We can't give up."

She stared straight ahead and cleared her throat nervously, then brought her hands down to her sides, clenching her fists. "Centuries are a drop in a bucket for the celestial, and he will never stop in his endeavor to bring this planet to ruin."

Kiami watched the pair as Amanda reached over and covered one of Emily's fists with her own hand before addressing everyone in the cave. "We will have to fight like the monsters he accuses us of being."

Emily turned her face to look at Amanda as she spoke again with more confidence. "We will have to fight like we will never die. This is our rally cry!"

Cheers erupted in the cave again, then sputtered to a halt as Justin hopped to his feet. "We will only be able to resist together!"

They yelled in unison, "Together!"

As if on cue, a sudden change in the air pressure around them caught Kiami's attention.

The wind picked up outside the cavern, emitting an eerie whistle as it breached the cave entrance.

She jumped up and moved toward the opening, lifting her face skyward as the others crowded around her.

When she had arrived, the sky was an unwavering pale blue that stretched out in every direction as far as she could see.

Now, above them, that blue was being pushed away and replaced by a rapidly spreading patchwork of vivid colors.

Emily stood on her toes and lifted her fist into the air. "It's time to move out!"

38

Amanda - Battlefield

The Human Realm

As she watched the pale blue sky dissolve, Amanda clutched the handle of her staff. She had seen the sky fill with such an array of brilliant colors before.

A gust blew her hair wildly around her face as she looked to her right and then left. Kiami and Emily were on either side of her. The others were behind them, still partially covered by the cave's mouth but exposed enough to understand this was no normal storm that approached.

The cave offered them cover from the impending onslaught of unpredictable weather, but they would easily be trapped and cornered inside, which was what she suspected the celestial was hoping for by causing a magical storm to begin with.

She stepped forward, expecting to lead the others away from the base camp, but found that Emily and Kiami both moved ahead with her as if they were a single entity.

For now, at least, they were in sync, she thought as she moved farther away with her head tilted down while she pushed through the increasing gusts.

A hand grasped at her forearm, and she raised her face to see Emily pointing ahead. As Kiami relaxed her grip, Amanda looked out at the two hazy figures in the distance.

She turned her head to make sure the others still followed, then looked beyond them to estimate their distance from the cave.

The wind was loud in her ears, and she fought to hear her own voice. "We should get farther from the cave. More toward the center of where the mountain stood!"

Kiami's hand dropped from her arm, and her voice rang out, "Straight at them then?"

The wind slowed around her, making the end of her question echo into the emptiness.

Still looking at her, Amanda nodded before once again facing forward, then motioned her companions to continue their advance.

Each step they took away from the cave seemed to provoke the celestial more, and after their next hasty burst onward, the rain began.

It came down hard and quick, ending after a few drenching seconds. The fresh mud beneath her feet made a squelching noise as she attempted to keep moving and pushing on.

This time, it was her turn to reach out her arms to stop the others. "We are far enough."

"Or close enough," Emily countered from her left, sounding breathy.

Amanda gave a nod. "We are far enough from the cave yet close enough to our attacker and his accomplice that they shouldn't be able to take us by surprise."

She sucked in the air around her until her lungs felt tight, then held it for several seconds before releasing it in a slow, controlled manner.

Kiami stepped closer, and Emily followed suit, closing the gap between them. "How long do you think he and his partner can keep this up?"

In truth, she didn't know the answer to Emily's question, so she shrugged it off as Justin, Etzion, Marise, and Blaine joined them in their huddle.

As they looked at her for instructions, it was Kiami that spoke up. "That is not his accomplice, but rather his prisoner."

Amanda lifted her face, squinting to try to make out the details that Kiami could see.

The shorter figure was in front. Long, dark hair hung down past its shoulders, and the being's hands seemed to be clasped in front.

"It is Jacqueline," Kiami added somberly. "Her hands are shackled."

The blood drained from Amanda's face. She could only assume the restraints were iron, which was poison to the jinni and would stop her from using her abilities to escape.

Everything she had done up to this point would be for nothing if the celestial managed to sway Kiami by using her guardian against her.

Amanda closed her eyes and took in another deep breath; it would mean that she had collapsed the mountain for nothing.

Emily moved in front of her. "Brace yourselves. They are coming."

39

Kiami - Northern Roost

The Human Realm

Kiami continued to watch their attacker and Jacqueline. They were still far enough away that the others couldn't make out the details of their faces, but she could.

As angry as she was at her guardian, she didn't wish her a fate such as Amanda's or worse. She wanted to morph into her owl form and rush to Jacqueline's aid, but she held her position and averted her eyes.

She stared down at the ground, wondering if she had been wrong to call out what she saw; her announcement wouldn't change anything. They needed to work together to wear the celestial down, pushing him to use his abilities until he changed into his nebula-like form.

Each of them had promised not to stray from the plan, no matter what the celestial threw at them, and at the moment that meant Marise was using his ability to form a loose circle around them.

The soaked dirt beneath her had become a symphony of rich and sweet browns, each of them brought to new intensity by the recent rain.

She tried to concentrate on that instead of the image of the pair that approached, but it was no use.

Even from this distance, the pale being beside her guardian looked otherworldly in his brightly colored cloak. The visible skin on his bald head shimmered beneath the light from above, accentuating his multicolored irises.

An arm slid around her waist, and Kiami raised her head. Her eyes locked on to Amanda's, and her friend said in a hushed voice, "Remember, the celestial is only flesh and blood."

She gulped, then mouthed, "*I know.*"

The celestial called out to them, "Is this what you want, Amanda? For me to keep hurting people that your friends care about?"

"You are a monster." Emily spat the words out as if she had a bad taste in her mouth.

The celestial let out a hearty chuckle. "Why? Because of the way I treat my daughters? They didn't follow instructions. Do you know how many children I have made? What if all of them went around creating worlds any which way they pleased? All this power was never meant to be placed in one planet!"

He rested one of his hands on his hips and continued, "Amanda, I thought we already cleared this up. You and your friends are the monsters in this scenario."

The celestial lifted his other hand and rolled his wrist in a circle as he explained, "We used to have a term for this on my planet, when it felt like you were reliving the same moment twice. I think it was *déjà vu* or something like that."

"You can't just go around creating then destroying planets and people!"

"That's an interesting thought, but it's wrong, wrong, wrong. The race I come from transcended those ideas long ago. We are scientists above all else."

Justin chimed in, "Yeah, and after what you have done, I'm sure the people of your world would welcome you home at any time, right?"

The celestial's nostrils flared as he continued. "They broke the rules. So I encouraged their creations to break the rules. I have been helping push for fights, whispering in the ears of the creatures. Plotting a spectacular end to this planet. You should keep in mind that it wasn't that hard to persuade my daughters' beloved creations to work against them, even after you moved to change the course."

"We know. The world caught fire, and you're the one that lit the spark. At least I have never claimed to be anything other than what I am. A tapestry of hate that you have woven."

"Amanda, why do you always have to learn the hard way? I can stop punishing you now; all you have to do is concede."

"We will do all we can to resist you until our last breath." Amanda pulled back her arm and wiped beads of sweat from her brow.

Kiami closed her eyes and steadied herself. The heat and humidity had been on the rise since the rain stopped. Kiami had barely made note of it, since the rapid change wouldn't affect her much, but she now realized the harm it could do to the others.

"Amanda, I can do this all day. Can your friends?"

They needed to move on to the next step. They needed to separate and attack from different angles so that he couldn't focus on all of them at once, but it wasn't her call to make.

She flinched as damp fuzz tickled the bare flesh of her heel. Then she released a relieved sigh as she looked down to see two tiny black eyes peering up at her amid a mess of fur.

Kiami bent down and scratched at Fizzle's head, but as she leaned farther in to scoop him up in her arms, he let out a low growl and backed away.

She furrowed her brow as he released another throaty growl. With it, his mess of fur seemed to stand up at attention all around his cantaloupe-shaped body.

She straightened and relaxed her features as she realized the critter wasn't focusing on her, but rather on what was happening in the distance.

Being a full head taller than her comrades, even with the ring of Marises that encircled them she had an unobstructed view of the celestial and his prisoner.

Jacqueline seemed subdued or in some sort of sleeping state. She stood back several feet from the celestial with her head bent down toward her chest, and her eyes appeared to be closed.

The celestial himself had stopped advancing about a hundred feet out and had drawn a sword that glowed a bright orange, which he waved menacingly above his head, taunting them. The hair at the back of her neck prickled at the sight of the weapon.

It was probably the reason Etzion hadn't gone forward, signaling the others to do the same.

Amanda had warned them about the sword that had taken her arm, but she hadn't thought he would brandish it before they even had a chance to separate and engage him. Given his ability to divert their magic, timing was everything.

Fizzle let out a shrill yip, then darted forward in a blur of dark brown movement.

She cried out, "NO, FIZZLE," but he didn't hesitate.

As he zeroed in on his target, his faced raised and his wide mouth opened, emitting a howl the likes of which Kiami had never heard before.

Her ears were so sensitive to the sound that she clapped her hands over them. To her amazement, hundreds of brown blurs appeared in the distance, as if called forth by their pack leader, all rushing at the celestial and creating a diversion.

The sword fell as he whipped around to engage the attack.

He lifted his hands in the air, and bright light shot upward from them toward the sky with a sharp crack, like reverse lightning.

The creatures yelped as pea-sized hail began to fall all round them.

Etzion's voice rose from behind them. "Now."

Kiami transformed as she pushed past the others, intent on meeting him on the other side of the celestial and her guardian. Yet she paused halfway, hovering above the attacker and his unflinching prisoner, watching the strange ballet of Fizzle and the many members of his species that had followed him into battle as they darted back and forth, circling around and then running straight at the aggressor. From the ground, their counterattack had seemed random, but from above the movements appeared rehearsed.

40

Emily - Eastern Post

The Human Realm

The small pieces of hail stung when they hit Emily's arms and face as she looked out at the sword that had sliced through Amanda's flesh with such heat that it had cauterized her wound even as it severed skin, muscle, and bone.

These bursts of extreme weather were daunting but short. The sword, on the other hand, seemed much more threatening.

Since the celestial had dropped the dangerous weapon, the metal's orange glow had faded, and Emily wondered if that meant it could be handled safely by one of them.

She looked around at her comrades, catching sight of Justin, who gave her a wink before he spun in a westward direction, running toward his post. They would be set up around the celestial like lines on a compass, with Blaine's wisps and Marise's copies filling in the gaps between.

Emily moved to her position at the east of the attacker, leaving Amanda where they had all grouped together. They had hoped this arrangement would prevent the celestial from using their own abilities against them.

Above them, Kiami had halted her forward movement and fanned her wings as she appeared to watch the activity below. Emily wondered if this was normal for an owl of her size but quickly shrugged it off. Magic seemed to make many things possible that otherwise wouldn't be completed so easily.

Emily looked across to see that Justin, with his arms ablaze, and Etzion, who moved in and out of sight around his post, were competing for the celestial's attention against the Fizzle-like critters.

Taking the sword had not been part of the plan, but she turned to the copy of Marise closest to her and voiced her concern about the weapon that lay on the ground near the celestial's feet. Like an odd game of telephone, his heads turned one after the other as he repeated her words in a low voice.

Several fist-sized wisps lifted from their posts and shot up into the air to get Kiami's attention, then dove down at the ground as if trying to get the point across as the silvery owl moved to follow.

As Kiami poised her claws to grab the hilt, a strong gust caused her to falter, missing her mark, and as she went careening to the ground, Emily realized the hail had stopped.

She looked up. Etzion had paused his movement. He watched, his mouth hanging open in horror, as the fire along Justin's arms lifted, swirling outward as if it was being pulled from his body by the celestial's powers.

Another gust blew past her, feeling warmer than the air around her. As it met the already spinning meter of fire, the intensity of its twisting grew, and the top opened like a funnel.

The fuzzy creatures all around the area seemed to yelp and whine in unison. She saw several balls of brown fluff fly at it as if sucked into the short, twisting vortex.

Although grateful for the help they gave, she hoped that the rest would flee as she took several instinctive steps backward. Unlike the furry creatures, running from the fiery tornado altogether was not an option for her.

Emily chewed at her bottom lip. *If he can't focus on the tornado, it will die.*

She searched the area for Kiami's owl form, but instead she found her in human form on her knees near Justin. Both were probably dazed and perhaps in shock, but since her healing ability wasn't calling for her to release it, she knew they weren't badly hurt.

Emily abandoned her post and darted toward the weapon.

41

Amanda - Sacrifice

The Human Realm

As far as Amanda could tell, all the critters that resembled Fizzle had either disappeared into the unknown or were swallowed up by the fire twister.

Even without their somewhat helpful although unruly presence, it was harder to keep track of everyone than Amanda first anticipated.

She had missed whatever led Kiami to dive for the sword the first time, but luckily she had spotted Emily as she took her chance, first running and then diving down to grab the hilt of the cooled metal.

She knew she wasn't the only one to notice as the tornado began to sputter, its crackling flames losing some of their intense heat as it swept passed her and away from the circle they had created.

She grasped at the wooden handle of her staff, ready to intervene, but even before her magic had a chance to accept her call, Etzion ran forward with his head bent down and his arms outstretched, aiming to tackle the celestial as if he was playing defense in a sporting event.

His back hit the ground with a thud, and he vanished. He reappeared at his post, and Amanda allowed her magic to seep from her and into her staff.

Emily's own eyes were wide as she hefted herself back to her feet, although she seemed oblivious to the fact that Etzion had just bought her more time. The hilt of the weapon was grasped within the fingers of one hand, but the weapon itself appeared to be too heavy for her to lift any higher, yet she seemed unwilling to leave it behind.

Once the celestial regained his composure and found his footing, he would reach her in no time.

The ground rumbled beneath Amanda as she let the wave of magic loose from her staff. She held her breath as the long, shadowy tendrils began to engulf him.

Kiami and Justin moved toward Emily, pulling her backward with such unexpected force that the weapon slid from her hand, landing back where it had been when the celestial first released it.

Amanda let out a sigh of relief, then sucked her breath in as she was pulled forward.

The tendrils of magic that had begun to overtake the celestial reversed direction, unwrapping as he stood.

The shadowy trails took on an inkier appearance as they were maneuvered and manipulated by his powers.

Amanda braced herself for his counterattack, but as the tendril moved out, Marise intercepted by sending his copies forward all at once, then drew them back into himself before the celestial could grab hold of the ability.

Jarred by the intrusion, the celestial relinquished control of her powers, and Amanda moved to change tactics as fast as she could.

Now, she thought of her time below the mountain that had once stood in this spot. She ground her teeth and pushed her magic to encircle herself as she had done to protect her body from the falling debris when it crumbled around her.

When he reached out to redirect her magic again, this time toward Marise, the stolen power inched away from her and reformed her protective shield around him.

For the first full minute of the onslaught, the celestial didn't seem to understand, then the tops of his flat rounded ears visibly reddened as he crinkled his nose in disgust and released her magic back to her control.

"You children only seem to understand one thing," he snarled, then reached forward with his right hand and spat out, "Destruction."

The sword levitated from the ground hilt first, and he moved his fingers around the handle and then lifted it into the air. As he did, the blade ignited once again with its sinister orange glow.

He brought the sword down, shifting it sideways as he spun in a circle.

Jacqueline's eyes popped open, and her face twisted as the glowing metal met her jinn flesh, then just as quickly she disappeared into a cloud of dust before Amanda could even anticipate the full extent of his reach.

Kiami cried out, an unintelligible sound that was so piercing and guttural, for a split-second Amanda thought the blade had somehow struck her too.

Her friend went down onto her knees and leaned forward, digging her nails into the dirt as the same sound escaped her throat again.

Amanda wanted to rush to her side, but the others had already joined her fallen form, and there was no way she could help but to continue.

A loud clap of thunder sounded above her, and the sky darkened as if night had fallen without warning, covering over the blanket of colors that had been visible within its depths only moments ago.

The celestial drove the tip of the sword into the ground in front of himself, and another louder bang of thunder sounded in the night sky.

His face was brick-red as he acknowledged her again. "If destruction is what you are after, it is what you will get. I will continue this until you and your friends cause the realms to unravel around us."

Amanda hesitated as she sucked in a breath. Mustering the courage to go on, she forced a sly smile onto her face as she sent her retort. "Do you see a breach here? The gems are stronger together! You're the only thing unraveling."

"We will see about that," he scoffed.

Amanda looked over at the others where they stood together. Even Blaine had finished reforming. "Get ready!"

The celestial turned toward them and shouted, "You can do nothing to me!"

Thunder rumbled above them once more, but this time the ground groaned beneath Amanda as well, and she glanced down at his feet.

A misty vapor, like fog, curled out from below him as he rose upward off the ground as if suspended from the dark side of the moon by an invisible tether.

As the others joined her side, the celestial's human flesh seemed to darken and melt into the background of the black sky for a brief moment, then his human-like outline reappeared in a burst of colors and twinkling lights.

This was it, their one chance. The very thing they had been waiting for.

42

Emily - Unbroken

The Human Realm

Emily watched alongside Amanda near her staff, which she had sank into the ground in much the same way she had when they were in the Emerald Mountains as their attacker morphed.

It was as if the celestial had sucked all the bright-colored patches of sky and cloud back into himself, and they had replaced his human visage. As his new form continued to expand, Emily could see things within the swirling clouds of smoke and debris that now made up his entire being, which she could only describe as moving dust particles, gasses, even stars of multiple shapes and sizes.

His new appearance reminded her of photos of nebulae in space that stretched out to be hundreds of light-years across, glowing with rich colors and swirls of light that included hues of bold reds, rich blues, teals, and luscious greens.

Emily gulped but reached for Amanda's staff, as she had been instructed when they went over the plan. Of course, overall things hadn't gone exactly as they had wished, she still held out the hope that if they wore the celestial down, the goddesses would appear to take him away for good.

She hadn't used her healing power since the battle began, and even if she had, Emily couldn't control the destructive magic that forced its way out of her after she repaired someone, so she doubted that her presence would be helpful to the cause.

She took in the rest of the sky. It remained pitch black beyond the celestial, and yet she swore something glinted far in the distance. She squeezed her eyes tight, then opened them again, searching the spot where she had thought the abnormality had occurred.

Emily cast her gaze back down and whispered, "Wishful thinking?"

She hadn't meant for anyone to hear her, but as Amanda's hand butted up against her own, then covered it, she was sure the gesture meant at least one person had.

Filled with a sudden resurgence of reassurance, she lifted her voice to address the others in an attempt to draw them closer. "I know it's hard, but we have to go on. Remember, we are stronger together, no matter your gift..."

When only a few halfhearted claps and grunts sounded around her, she tried again. "This is how we rise up, together! It's our world. They can never have it!"

Amanda's hand twitched over her own, and Emily looked back up at her comrades as they silently drew nearer.

They looked haggard and worn. Their clothing, although dried within minutes after the downpour that had soaked them through, now hung from their bodies, covered in grime and sweat. The dirt beneath their feet had become mud, then dried to the sole of their shoes, or in Kiami's case, all the way up her calves.

Etzion, whose exposed forearm was welted and swelling, also toted a fat lip, which she thought must have bled at some point, since his chin was smeared with blood.

All of them seemed to be focused on the celestial, waiting for him to do something.

She felt a hand clamp onto her shoulder and glanced over it to see Justin had rooted himself between her and Amanda before reaching out to let her know he was there.

She gave him a meek half smile, then averted her gaze as Marise called out, "What's that?"

He pointed one finger out at the celestial's form and bellowed, "In his midsection."

Emily furrowed her brow as she stared hard at the bright blue circular region that seemed to be expanding across the area that would represent his stomach if he were in human form. The very center of the shape seemed to be turning darker and pulsating more rapidly by the second.

Amanda called over her shoulder, "Just be ready..."

Justin finished with a hint of sarcasm, "For anything. We know."

The being lifted his swirling arms midway, then a sharp swoosh rushed past Emily from behind, pulling her toward the celestial.

She tightened her grip, dug her feet into the ground, and squeezed her eyes shut.

Emily could hear the others cry out as they were pulled forward. She felt the staff jerk, then Amanda's hand lifted. The staff jerked again but remained planted.

She opened her eyes.

A mess of dirt and loose debris blurred her vision as it rushed past.

She squinted and tried to make out the shapes around her. Justin had managed to grab on to the bottom of the staff with both hands. He lay on his stomach, stretched feet first toward the vacuum.

Amanda still held tight with one hand, but she stood sideways with her other arm outstretched as her fingers grasped onto Marise's wrist.

She didn't see Etzion, Kiami, or Blaine. She gulped, then fluttered her eyelids, trying to rewet her rapidly drying eyes.

A sharp popping noise seemed to echo all around them, followed by a ghastly roar.

Justin let out a shriek as the ground below them rumbled and shifted. The swoosh of the air around them died down as the pull of the vacuum weekend, and Emily loosened her grip to allow her aching hands a brief reprieve as she tried to see what was happening.

It appeared as though the celestial had pivoted to the side, preoccupied by something else.

She righted herself as Amanda pulled Marise closer.

Justin crawled forward but kept his hand firmly attached to the staff.

"This is our chance." Amanda croaked the words out.

"Where are the others?"

Etzion appeared beside her. "Here."

He shot her a quick toothy smile then added, "It will take Blaine a moment to reform. Kiami is with the rest. She will be here."

"The rest?" Amanda asked.

"There's not much time to explain. They won't be able to distract him for very long."

Emily let out a sigh of relief. Jacqueline must have made it to the Chaos realm or to Bloise before she was captured. Either way, whoever it was, their intervention had probably saved them, for now at least.

When the fingers that groped Amanda's staff began to tingle, Emily knew she had called to her shadow magic, and she reached for the gem at the end of her own wand with the opposite hand.

43

Amanda - Black Hole

The Human Realm

"The rest?"

Time was not on their side, so Amanda hadn't waited for the others to get into position before she called to her magic. Emily and Justin were already connected to her through the staff, and she could feel their strange magic mingling with her own before she could see it.

Marise and Etzion each placed a hand on her shoulder, and a shudder ran through her when a sharp tingle made its way up her spine.

The black tendrils of her magic seemed to flicker as their gems' powers were added into the mix. Her heart hammered in her ears, and her chest felt heavy as Blaine's power began to seep in as well, but she concentrated on the celestial's form, determined to remain steadfast.

A whoosh, like the sound of ocean waves lapping on the shore, filled her ears. She gritted her teeth as Kiami's owl flew by close enough for her to make out, yet still seeming out of focus even as the bird turned back to land.

A cold chill ran through her, and she shivered despite the beads of sweat that had formed on her brow.

Moments later, goosebumps erupted along her arms and legs as the final half-bloods' magic entered the mix. She opened her eyes as wide as she could, but the world around her only became fuzzier. Knowing she couldn't keep this up, she pushed the mingled magic forward and out through her staff with all her might.

The hazy celestial roared as the power moved out and engulfed him.

The sound in her ears got louder, as if the waves were now crashing against a rocky shore, and the tight feeling in her chest increased, causing her to gasp for breath.

44

Kiami - Their Here

The Human Realm

The combined magic that the staff unleashed burst out, going forth like a strange piebald rainbow that rushed forward and then into the angered celestial. The sight had come as such a shock that she recoiled in sheer astonishment.

He only had time to let out one infuriated roar as the magic seemed to wash away his transformation, returning him to human form and forcing him to the ground. Once down, a loud noise, like the sound of a cracking whip, reverberated overhead.

It had happened so fast, the fact that he and Amanda had almost crumpled in unison could have gone undetected had they not all been within arm's reach of one another.

Kiami felt a scream rise up in her throat at the sight, but only air escaped her lips. No audible sound followed. She urged her body forward to join Emily at their friend's side, but other than her eyes, her voluntary muscles refused to obey her.

She roved the area with her sight and realized none of the others were moving either. Marise and Etzion stood in front of her, each with an arm outstretched toward their fallen comrade, as if they were posing for a painting.

She moved her eyes over the area where the celestial had fallen. Her head was tilted sideways at an angle, making it hard to take in the full picture. A beam of white light shot down to the spot he had landed, only now his limp body rose up within it, as if pulled by the force of the light itself.

She followed the light upward. The spacecraft's underbelly from which the light emanated looked roughly rectangular, with edges that appeared to be seamless and soft.

Its shape and texture felt somehow familiar, yet out of place against the blackened backdrop of the sky. She moved her eyes back onto the beam as the celestial came up to, then disappeared within the alien vessel without a visible door or hatch opening. The light of the beam did the same, vanishing from sight as if a switch was flicked off somewhere inside.

A blood-curdling scream she recognized as her own erupted in front of her, as if it had been suspended then released. Her hands rose to her throat, and she moved several steps forward all at once.

Her foot hit something, and she tilted down toward it, falling to the ground with her palms open in front of her. She pushed herself back up, making it to her knees just as a blue flare sputtered to life at one end of the craft. For a moment the ship seemed to propel silently closer with its front tilted skyward, a blue trail following behind as it proceeded. As the sound of a cracking whip reverberated overhead once more, the spacecraft disappeared from view.

She looked out after the ship into the darkness until stars began to emerge. A pained groan from somewhere nearby reminded her of Amanda and brought her back from her stupor.

She forced herself to look away and spun around to help her companions. Her eyes widened in shock as she saw Emily, Justin, and Marise carrying a limp Amanda away.

She ran toward them, arms flailing. "Where are you going?"

Emily grunted. "Back to the cave."

"We don't want to be here if they decide to return," Justin added.

"But she's..."

"Hurt," Emily groaned.

"Where's Etzion, Blaine?" Kiami stammered.

Justin lifted his chin up and out. "They went to see if there were survivors."

Kiami had forgotten about them. The humanoids from the Chaos realm had appeared as she was fleeing the suction of the vacuum the celestial had created. Luckily for her, she had been in owl form already, or she may not have managed so easily to escape the pull.

When she had first spotted them, she thought they were monsters coming to attack. Creatures that had slipped through a breech in the realms or that the celestial had summoned. She had already been through one battle that included similar rat-like humanoids to the pair she learned called themselves Howin and Dhruv. From a distance the handful of others that accompanied them didn't look much friendlier either.

As she approached, however, she realized Etzion and Blaine had found the entourage first and soon scolded herself for being so quick to judge as she worked to assist them in capturing the tyrant's attention. Without their help, things may have been even worse.

She ran toward the cave to catch up with Amanda's escorts. If nothing else, she needed to know that they had shown up.

Kiami had caught up with them just in time to take Emily's place. Her healing magic was already trying to force its way out, and she struggled to keep it at bay, causing herself real pain that showed not only on her pale face, but also in the way her movements had become jerky and stiff. Justin went to Emily's side to offer added support as she continued the walk.

Kiami leaned in as she took hold of Amanda, carrying her the rest of the way into the cave with Marise's help.

As they laid her on the ground within its walls, she whispered into her ear, "Howin, Dhruv, Kaelah, Bly, they were all here. And more too."

Amanda's eyelids fluttered but didn't open as a low groan escaped her.

Justin laid a hand on her shoulder. "Back up, Kiami."

As she pushed herself away, Emily moved to sit beside their wounded friend.

Emily glanced over her shoulder, revealing her red and puffy eyes, then she leaned in over Amanda and released her magic.

The hazy wave rolled out of her and over their still friend in a torrent, then dissipated as it extended past her body.

Emily pushed herself up and wrapped her arms around her stomach. "Is she okay?"

The healer whispered from her seat on the ground, "She is still alive, if that's what you mean."

Emily placed her hand on Amanda's head and pushed back her hair. "We started something. I want to finish. You need to be there. I can see a world that's waiting for us. We have the power to change everything. We will be the engineers and the designers."

Amanda's lips parted, and a wheeze rose from her chest. Emily leaned in, and Kiami moved closer to the pair. Her eyelids fluttered again, then opened in thin slits, but as she began to mutter, a dry cough rattled its way out, making most of her words sound like unintelligible nonsense.

A low groan pushed its way out, then she attempted to speak once more. The few words that managed to escape were barely above a whisper. "You healed my heart. You know I tried..."

When the words died away, Kiami bent forward and gave her a light kiss on the cheek. "I won't lose you too."

Heat radiated against her lips as they brushed against Amanda's flesh. It felt as if the sincerity in her own words faltered as her thoughts shifted to Jacqueline. Numbness washed over her. She had already grieved her loss long ago. Now she felt only guilt about the anger that boiled within her.

Unlike Amanda's motives, she would never understand her guardian's. She crossed her arms over her chest and tried to keep her voice stable as she sat back up and refocused her attention on her friend's prone form. "You just need to rest."

Amanda seemed to tremble in response, then her eyes widened with the effort as she forced the words out. "Let me go. I am tired of falling asleep in my own tears."

Emily jumped up, startling her as she moved toward the entrance of the cave, as if their friend's words were a knife aimed at her, threatening to stab into her flesh.

Kiami glanced into Amanda's vacant eyes, then pushed herself up to her feet to follow the healer to the opening.

Kiami caught sight of a silent tear that rolled down Emily's cheek, but the healer didn't flinch or look away from the horizon as she addressed her.

"What is it?"

"She isn't going to get better if she doesn't want to."

"Why would you say something like that?"

"The first thing she said to me, before you got close enough to hear was, 'I can't recall the last time I opened my eyes to see the world as a beautiful place. I used to."

Kiami's fists clenched. "She's in pain and delirious."

Emily shifted on her feet as she whispered back, "Maybe."

45

Emily - Bloise

The Human Realm

Emily had felt it just as she felt the thundering of her heart deep in her chest ... the moment that Amanda made her choice. The choice she hoped would save Sumir. She had tried to give herself to save them all.

Kiami thought she was delirious, but she didn't know the rest of what Amanda had said, and now the words echoed within Emily's head: *The longer I go on, the more I lose sight of what I was looking for to begin with.*

She cursed herself for not stopping her from taking in the combined magic. She had noticed how white her skin had become even with the mixture of mud and dirt from the ground that caked it, creating deep lines that almost looked like cracked porcelain across her exposed face and arms. Then, when the ship had appeared, Emily hadn't felt the pull ... and an ache had filled her. The weight of it was unbearable. She tried to move it, but like her body, it wouldn't budge, even though she knew Amanda wasn't dead. From her frozen position, she had been able to see how her lips remained parted a fraction of an inch and her chest rose slowly, then sank again.

It had been the worst feeling she ever suffered from, and it still lingered. Emily feared that if Amanda didn't return to them as she was before the fight, she would never be rid of it.

She took a step out beyond the portal, and as Kiami moved to follow, she turned back and shook her head. She needed to be alone for a moment.

Once she was sure her friend wouldn't continue, she moved farther from the cave entrance, closed her eyes, and screamed into the night.

When she opened them again, a familiar face looked back at her. As his silvery robes glinted in the starlight, Emily frowned.

Dimples appeared on Bloise's cheeks when he grinned. "That happy to see me, huh?"

Emily inhaled deeply, then let the breath out in slow, controlled bursts, trying to rid her voice of the irritation she felt at his late arrival. "Why are you here?"

His grin widened, causing crow's feet to radiate from the corners of his eyes. "For the incursion of course!"

Emily's frown deepened. "The celestials are gone."

"Oh, I know that, silly girl."

His eyes seemed to gleam as he continued, looking down at her.

"Long ago, when Amanda first encountered Jacob, I warned her that something else was coming. I even promised her I would be prepared."

Emily's throat constricted as the truth began to unravel. Her pulse quickened, causing her heartbeat to thunder in her ears. She raised her voice over the drumming. "You knew what was coming?"

"Thankfully, the four of you that visited me last gave me exactly what I needed to take control after they abandoned the planet. You follow?"

Emily's cheeks warmed as she recalled their visit to the old wizard. "And what exactly did we give you?"

"Well," his lips parted, showing off his yellowed teeth, "you gave me access to your gifts, of course. Nasty business, borrowing magical abilities. I shouldn't have done it. I vowed not to do such things again, but sometimes the temptation is just too strong."

Emily balled her fists at her sides. "That was your plan, to wait for us to do the hard work so you could get a shot at taking over?"

He shrugged. "You can't blame an old wizard for trying."

Emily tried to feel for the rebound magic that always accumulated after she healed someone, but although she could feel its pressure starting to bloom within her, it wasn't strong enough for her to yank free yet.

The wizard must have read her intent within her scrunched up features, because he leaned down, lifting a flame-filled hand toward her as he did. "And since I know Amanda isn't up for making an appearance, I think you might want to go have a meeting with your friends before you overreact, dearie."

He winked down at her, then lifted his other hand, revealing a shadowy tendril that wrapped around his wrist, then snaked up the sleeve of his robe toward his scrawny bicep.

Emily spun away from him and darted back toward the cave.

As she reached the entrance, her stomach twisted, bringing her to a stop. She bent forward with her hands on her knees as she swallowed and released several deep breaths.

"Emily?"

She lifted her face toward the voice to see Justin looking at her with fresh concern plastered on his features.

"Bloise is here," she answered, righting herself and looking around the interior of the cave to take in the reactions of her companions.

Marise sat upon one of the natural stone outcroppings with his legs crossed beneath him and his eyes fixed on his lap, as if he remained unfazed by the news, or her words had not been harsh enough to penetrate his thoughts.

In contrast, Etzion and Blaine looked back at her with uncertainty from where they stood near the center with Kiami. It appeared that the other half-bloods had returned from their search for survivors alone.

Justin rested a hand on his hip, then cocked one of his eyebrows. "A little late to the party, isn't he?"

"He showed up exactly when he meant to," Emily seethed. "He plans to hit us while we are at our weakest."

"Let him try," Justin quipped.

Emily shook her head at him. "It's no laughing matter."

"After all we have faced, you don't think we can stop one rogue wizard?"

She took a few weary steps toward him before speaking again. "He has access to your natural gifts, Justin. As well as mine, Kiami, and Amanda's. We gave him what he needed to borrow our magic. It was his plan all along, his way to be prepared to take over."

Justin folded his arms over his chest. "Well if we can't stop his incursion, who will?"

Kiami spoke up. "We can manage it with Etzion, Blaine, and Marise. He doesn't have access to their abilities..."

Marise cleared his throat as he rose from his seat. "About that. I may have left out part of the reason I left my family,"

Emily shifted on her feet. "So, he can use your ability too?"

The corners of his mouth were drawn downward as he sputtered a response. "I think so. I'm sorry."

Her eyes latched onto his, but he pulled them away, casting them down onto the floor, then began to wring his hands together as he continued. "Bloise promised to go away and leave my family alone, and he didn't make it sound like I had an option…"

"It's okay, Marise. Take a deep breath."

Justin bounded toward her. The almost jovial eagerness he had expressed moments ago was gone. "How can you say that? We are tired, hurt, hungry, angry. We are in no shape to go another round, Em."

"We need to stay clear-headed. Amanda knows the most about Bloise, and she is in no shape to fight," she scolded.

Etzion stood up and raised his hand as if he was waiting to be called on by a teacher. As she acknowledged him, he added, "Let's not forget trapped, if he followed you back here."

She grasped at Justin's arm as his reddening face turned in Marise's direction. "Steady. We have all had similar encounters. We have all had to make choices to keep ourselves and our loved ones safe. And your anger, Justin, is just what Bloise is hoping for. Just like the celestial, he's trying to distract us by making us argue amongst ourselves."

"And," Kiami added sternly, "before the battle, we all agreed that it would be up to us to keep leaders like the celestial from taking control again. We knew something like this could happen sooner or later."

Justin stomped his foot in frustration but stayed where he was as Emily nodded in agreement at the shapeshifter.

"K…" The single letter sounded from where Amanda lay on the cave floor.

"Me?" Kiami asked as she raised a hand to her chest and moved toward her.

Emily looked up at Justin, pleading with her eyes for him to let it go as she removed her hand from his arm. He closed his eyes and exhaled, nodding. When she was sure he wouldn't continue, she moved to join Kiami at Amanda's side.

"Give Bloise the kiss he was so interested in back at the dance."

"What?" Kiami recoiled, backing into Emily.

Amanda pushed herself onto one of her elbows. "Wait."

As Kiami moved toward her once again, Emily stepped to the side before advancing.

"He has your inherited song. He does not have access to your moonstone." Amanda closed her eyes and took in a haggard breath that wheezed back out before continuing, "Remember the boy on the beach."

Emily watched as Kiami's face fell. Then she lifted her hand and clutched the moonstone at her throat, turned, and headed for the entrance of the cave.

When she moved to follow, Kiami stopped as if waiting for her to catch up. Once she was within arm's reach, Kiami spoke up. "Emily, some things are meant to be done alone."

"No, Kiami. You don't need to be alone. And what if he knows how the gem affects your powers? What if he resists?"

46

Kiami - A Kiss on the Lips

The Human Realm

Alone would be better. Kiami closed her eyes as the thought settled in.

She knew the memory of the morning she had received her gemstone was tainted by her own self-loathing, but still she didn't fight it as a corrupt version of the events filled her subconscious.

The picturesque sunrise and clear, lapping waves she had ventured out to enjoy after she harnessed the gift morphed into violent bursts of water that crashed against the shore while a gloomy sky filled with grays and blacks loomed overhead.

As the echo of herself made its way down the beach and caught sight of the sandy-haired boy. It paused in its procession to lick its lips in anticipation of what was to come.

She winced and released her grip on the moonstone as a shudder ran through her. Even though the memory was inaccurate, the ending would still be the same. She would kiss the boy, and he would age, similar to how Jasmine had when she had removed the opal necklace, only for him the process wouldn't stop until he disintegrated in her arms.

Kiami hadn't thought much about the incident in a long time, at least not after Amanda admitted to having witnessed it in one of her visions.

She lifted her index finger to her lips and began chewing at the nail as renewed shame washed over her, just as a wave would wash over the shore of the beach below her childhood home.

She hadn't known what would happen when she kissed the innocent bystander, stealing his life, even so the fact remained ingrained in her that after she understood what was happening, she hadn't been able to stop it.

She didn't want any of the other half-bloods to witness a display of her losing control. She was, after all, the calm and optimistic one, and it would highlight a part of her that she had never wanted to come to the surface.

Blaine had already witnessed so much, if Kiami was going to have to be escorted, she figured the being would be the least affected. In fact, for all she knew, one of the wisps could have trailed her to the beach that day and seen what happened anyway.

Kiami opened her eyes and looked up into Emily's. "Blaine can join me in wisp form. That way if something goes wrong, more of you can be summoned quickly."

"Just because Bloise can use our gifts, it doesn't mean we would be helpless in a fight against him," Emily argued as she crossed her arms over her puffed-out chest.

Kiami countered, unwavering in her stance, "We cannot leave Amanda unprotected."

Emily shot back sternly, "Marise can stay with her. He is quick on his feet and can cause a decent diversion with his ability."

"What if Bloise uses my song against you, forcing you to attack me? Or uses Justin's fire to hurt you?" Kiami shook her head. "None of you deserve the guilt that would come with that."

Etzion's voice rose from where he stood, the volume increasing in intensity with each question. "What if you do it first? Take control of us, I mean? Would he be able to weasel his way into our heads if you're already in there?"

Kiami watched as Emily's eyes widened at the suggestion, then she clapped her hands as she exclaimed, "Brilliant idea, Etzion!"

"We can't be sure that would stop him," Kiami countered, dismissing the suggestion.

Emily's face reddened. "Since when has that stopped you in the past? I think Etzion could be on to something."

"I am just not fond of the idea, okay?" Kiami felt deflated.

"Noted. But if you sing and direct us to fight, we will, correct?"

Her head jerked at an awkward angle as she nodded.

"Then it's settled," Emily announced. "Marise can stay with Amanda, and we will join you, compelled by your song."

Justin moved forward, wringing his hands. "Em?"

"What, Justin? Your tired?"

Emily spat the words out as if they caused a bad taste in her mouth. "You can stay behind here with Marise too then."

His eyebrows pulled close together as he dropped his hands to his sides and balled them into fists. "Who's being hotheaded now?"

Emily flung her arms up. "How do you think Amanda feels? Lying there in pain and listening to us argue over something we already agreed to? This fight between good and evil is far from over. We need to remove Bloise from the equation, or everything we accomplished by ridding Sumir of the celestial will be for nothing."

The conviction in Emily's voice caused Kiami to take a step back. She wasn't going to drop it. They were coming with her to face the wizard, no matter what.

Maybe, she thought, *if I manage to keep them compelled, I can send them away before they witness the end I have in store for Bloise.*

As the others gathered outside the cover of the cave, Kiami hesitated. She spun toward the back, where Amanda lay covered to her chin by a mud-splattered cloak.

Marise squirmed in discomfort as he looked up from where he sat beside the courier of shadow magic. "No one will disturb her."

He glanced back down at Amanda, then lifted his face again, catching her gaze once more. He raised his hand in a salute. "I promise."

Kiami shot him a half smile then turned back to the opening, where Etzion stood. He seemed to be waiting for her, and as she stepped outside, he reached for her shoulder.

When their eyes met, the sapphire flecks around his irises twinkled back at her, but his lips were drawn inward. "I'm sorry."

She shook her head and raised her own hand to cover his. "No. It was a good suggestion."

"That doesn't make me any less sorry for the turmoil it caused. I can see that it's not what you wanted, and those two," he said, gesturing to Emily and Justin with his free hand, "still seem pretty agitated with one another."

Kiami released his hand, and as it dropped to his side, she shrugged. "It's been a long road."

She moved to step past him but paused as he spoke again. "Kiami."

"Yeah?" She peered back over her shoulder at him.

"Would it make you feel better if you considered that Bloise may have been the one to raise the flag about Jacqueline to the celestial?"

"What Bloise did or didn't do isn't what makes me hesitant. It is what I could become when I do what is necessary to end him. That's what bothers me."

47

Amanda - Vision

The Human Realm

Amanda's flesh felt clammy beneath the cloak Etzion had thrown over her in his haste to stop the onslaught of chills that had caused her to writhe in discomfort. She was sure, had he known her skin burned against the added pressure, he wouldn't have done it.

Racked with pain and helpless to do anything other than listen as the others argued, in her current state Amanda could scarcely keep her thoughts straight. She was lucky she had managed to speak even the few words she had sputtered to Kiami.

Marise had moved close enough that she could make out the outline of his shape through her slitted eyes, but as she tried to force them wider, her vision was blotched with violent colors that seemed to shift without a pattern.

She didn't feel ill will toward him for the choice he had made. They had all done things under duress that they regretted.

She swallowed hard, causing pins and needles to radiate from her throat, then gritted her teeth and willed her eyes to close again. As the light faded, the weight deep in her chest seemed to lift, and black dots began to swim around behind her eyelids, darting back and forth. She clenched them tighter, preparing for delirium to take hold.

As she gave in, little by little the pain seemed to dissipate, then the sensation of the rough cloak over her and the solid ground beneath her disappeared.

Her senses sharpened all at once. The musty cave air had been replaced by an earthy scent that carried undertones of pine and ozone.

Her first thought was that she had slept through her friends' return, and they had carried her from the cave so that she could breathe fresh air.

Like a lightning bolt hurtling through the sky, the name "Bloise" flashed in her mind. Her focus had seemed to return, then amplify. She scolded herself for not preparing the others better for an encounter with the wizard. Deep down, she had known he had it in him to do something like this, but she had allowed herself to be blinded by the hope that once the celestial was gone, they would have a reprieve from such things.

As she opened her eyes, muddled thoughts seeped in from multiple directions, as if the act had caused her thoughts to splinter and scatter.

Just as unsettling was what she saw when she focused ahead. Instead of one clear picture, she saw five shard-like sections laid out in front of her, like she was meant to glue them back together to make a whole.

In four of the images Etzion, Justin, Emily, and Kiami were poised for attack, yet all four swayed in time to a sweet melody she couldn't quite grasp on to. The sensation that she was standing beside each of them and flanking Bloise on all sides felt wrong, yet that was what she saw. Beside her, Kiami stood, staring Bloise in the eye as she continued to hum that sweet melody. Yet also beside her, Justin was staring at the back of the wizard's silvery cape...

Amanda averted her attention to the fifth shard, where her partially obscured view started just above Marise's head. In the image, he sat on the cave floor, staring down with a concerned expression. Beside him, a shrouded figure was lying flat. The only visible feature was the young woman's pale face and matted hair.

She wanted to scream as the realization dawned on her. It had not been delirium that took her, but a vision. One unlike any she had had before. Her previous experiences had always been singular, through one of the other half-blood's eyes. Instead, she was seeing what was happening the way Blaine would, in wisp form.

The images reflecting back at her reminded her of looking out one of the slender windows in the tower of Jacob's castle, though the balls of energy didn't really have eyes in the scene she did. Lucky for her, he had only separated into five wisps. Any more and Amanda didn't think she could manage to keep track. The experience already felt fragmented and unbalanced.

Her new understanding meant that her initial impression was backward. The thoughts she was experiencing seemed unfocused because they were coming at her from opposing directions.

Even though Blaine was one being, the individual ideas from each wisp instance started out separate then made its way back to the figurative base to be rejoined as one, creating the being's unified consciousness when in this energy form.

She heard herself groan from the fifth visual fragment. Amanda glanced over at the pair, watching as Marise leaned forward and placed the back of his hand on her head to check her temperature as she muttered. Amanda had never seen herself when she was viewing the world from a host's eyes. Knowing Marise would have no idea a vision had overtaken her, she huffed at the sight. "Well, I know I am still alive."

With the understanding came the realization that there was yet another difference in this experience from the rest. She felt nothing in the way of shame, fear, anger, or excitement emanating from this host. In the past as a passenger, she had always felt her hosts' emotions, as if their mental state was transferred to her.

She pulled her eyes away to focus her attention on the other four shards, where it appeared that Kiami was having a discussion with Bloise, only no matter how animated their faces became, she heard nothing.

Another oddity of this experience, she thought as she took in her partitioned view around the attacker. Within her view of Justin, she could see flames had risen upon his shoulders, but his face remained blank as he continued his melodic swaying in unison with the other three.

To the right of Bloise, Etzion clutched his sapphire gemstone. From the side view of his face, his lips appeared to be pulled back in what could have been either a smile or a snarl. On the right, Emily's wand was gripped in one hand and pointed out at the wizard. While Amanda watched her sway, her face suddenly wrinkled up as if she was in pain and holding back a scream as it tried to wrench itself loose.

Amanda's brow furrowed. *Emily is holding her own rebound magic at bay because like Etzion and Justin, Kiami is controlling her with her song.*

With Blaine in his wisp state and Bloise having borrowed his own variation of Kiami's song, Amanda wondered if both were immune to its melody.

She made a conscious effort to ignore the other images as she locked her eyes onto the instance of Kiami, focusing all her attention on the wisps' view from beside her.

Kiami's eyes were locked in front of her, staring at the glowing ball of orange and yellow fire that the wizard threatened her with.

Bloise's eyebrows rose, and his upper eyelids lowered slightly as he seemed to wind up his arm for the attack.

A rush of skepticism surrounded Amanda, as if her senses had been dulled by her lack of concentration. A snicker sounded, then Bloise's voice sang out, sounding smug as it broke through her bubble of silence. "How hard do you think it would be for me to interrupt the hold you have on your friends and take over, dearie?"

He hurled the ball forward, and fear beat at her from every angle even as she saw Kiami step easily out of its path.

Seeming unfazed, Kiami cocked her head to the side. "You have it all wrong, silly wizard. I am holding them back from attacking you so that we can have a civilized conversation."

"Is that so? I think you're bluffing." As he spoke the last word, a tendril of inky dark magic began to snake its way out from the clay directly below him, as if he was pulling her dark magic from the ground at his feet.

Kiami seemed to disregard the threat altogether. "You don't have what it takes to control this world. But together..." she folded her arms over her chest nonchalantly, "we could accomplish amazing things."

Amanda was reminded of her time with Jacob and how he had tried to get her to join him in his quest for power. Had she told Kiami that story? She couldn't quite remember, but she hoped her friend spoke with false sincerity, even as confusion and disbelief batted at her from

Blaine. Jacob had been trying to make her feel inadequate, like her only choice had been to accept his offer, but she had seen past his bluff.

The tendril of dark magic had made its way to Bloise's midsection, and he reached for it, allowing his fingers to run through the substance. "I don't believe you."

A sudden screech echoed from beside them, and he spun on his heels, pushing the dark magic out as he moved. Before the tendril could reach its target, a wave of energy burst forward, knocking the inky magic back at the wizard and forcing him onto his knees.

Kiami dropped her arms at her sides. "I warned you. Just because you borrowed the power doesn't mean you can handle it."

Concerned about what the rapid release of Emily's rebound magic would do to her while she was under Kiami's control, Amanda had to force herself not to look for Emily in the other shards. She needed to concentrate on what was happening between the wizard and Kiami.

A small gasp of relief seemed to flutter at her, and she took it as a sign that Emily was fine. Still, fear lingered, exuding from her host's strange mind in bursts.

Kiami smiled, then tapped her foot on the ground.

Pleased with her own cleverness, Amanda thought as Kiami spoke again.

"I can send them away right now. Once you admit that you need me. Then we can seal the deal."

A knot formed within Amanda's consciousness. It was all too parallel to what she had experienced at the start of her journey. Except this time it was Kiami allowing the darkness in. Something she never thought she would live to see.

Bloise pushed himself up to his feet. "Fine. Send them away." The statement sounded more like a threat than an admittance that he needed her help, and Amanda wanted to look away once more. She knew exactly what Kiami had in store for him, and although she had made the suggestion, she didn't realize the effect it would have on her friend.

Kiami's lips curled back in a cruel smile as her melody shifted. The change was slight, but Amanda was concentrating so hard on the scene that she heard the shift right away. Again, she pleaded with herself not to look.

"They are leaving." Kiami winked and took a step toward the wizard.

The wizard didn't move away, only looked at her coyly. *Perhaps*, Amanda thought, *he was under the impression that her guard was down*, but Amanda knew otherwise. She had seen firsthand what happened to the boy on the beach. She had seen the look in Kiami's eyes when she realized what was happening and that she couldn't stop it.

"Let's bind this partnership with a kiss."

Amanda watched as Kiami wrapped an arm around the wizard's shoulder and moved in for the kiss, then she finally allowed herself to look away. The sound around her vanished as she allowed her focus to spread out. But Blaine's wisps had not retreated with the others, and instead of being spared the old wizard's end, she had a brief glimpse of the whole scene before everything went dark.

In that instance, it wasn't Bloise's crumpling form that bothered her the most; it was the hollow way Kiami's eyes seemed to stare ahead, her concentration unwavering. They looked like deep, unrelenting pools.

48

Kiami - Starry Eyed

The Human Realm

Kiami had been watching Emily closely during the fight. Given her increased agitation before they left the cover of the cave, she knew it would only be a matter of time before the countereffects of her attempt at healing Amanda would force their way out. She had only hoped the threat from the discharge would be enough to scare the wizard into submission.

She hadn't wanted any of them to witness the end she had given to Bloise, and she was glad that only Blaine had. Overall, she had found it pretty easy to entice the wizard with her kiss, and in the end he had disintegrated much faster than the poor boy on the beach, but the simplicity of the act had not made it any easier for her to bear.

Kiami had tried to tell herself she had only managed to accomplish what felt to her to be an unthinkable thing, out of necessity, but deep down she no longer thought it was true, and the change made her feel discontented and curious.

While the other half-bloods seemed to be complacent in their current stations, she looked longingly up at the sky. Being created from a direct line of celestial heritage, she couldn't help but wonder if she really belonged here on Sumir at all anymore.

Deep down, she was sure that the other celestial beings could offer her an explanation as to why she was so different than the trio of goddesses whose realm she represented, and she wanted to understand their motives, that thirst for advancement that had driven the celestial people, her people, to go to such lengths.

She often wondered about the wall of twinkling lights below the Chaos realm, and whether or not any of the remaining watch posts had ships, like the one the goddesses had used to take their father through the stars.

Kiami had tried to discuss the blooming desires and metamorphosis in herself with Amanda, but since they had left the fallen mountain, preoccupied by her own agenda, Amanda seemed unwilling to help Kiami uncover more of her otherworldly history.

In fact, Amanda had spent most of her time within the black tower of the Emerald Mountains. As far as Kiami could tell, the strange spire remained abandoned, though her friend seemed unwavering in her idea that the guardian who had once resided there would return, and she was determined to be there when it did.

Despite the chasm she felt growing between herself and the others, Kiami smiled. One day she would be free of the gem's burden, and she would find out exactly where the celestial people had come from.

About the Author

M. Ainihi is a passionate Dark Fantasy Author, proud Mother, Wife, and Adventurer. She hails from the wilds of Upstate New York and currently residing in the Chicagoland area.

You can connect with me on:
- https://www.concealedrealms.com
- https://twitter.com/m_ainihi
- https://goodreads.com

Also by M. Ainihi

Rise: A Blood Inheritance Novel

Most humans do not know about the existence of the outer realms, or the fierce battles that once waged between the magical races before their creation. But for teen Amanda, ever since she encountered the jinni in the forest, it's her new reality, a place where darkness lies around every corner, and she's lost almost all hope of surviving it.

Lost: A Blood Inheritance Novel

Before Amanda knew about the seven realms, she longed to know her mother. Now her inherited gift is the very thing she fears most, and even as she fights to keep the shadow magic at bay, she can feel it growing inside her. Plagued by nightmares and haunted by a new vision of Emily, a cryptic accusation may just send her tumbling over the edge.

Endow: A Blood Inheritance Novel

Endow takes Amanda, Emily, and Kiami on a dangerous trip through the realms. Amanda is determined to prove that the stones they were given are the very ones from the ancient myth. To do so she may have to divulge a few of her dark secrets.

The Warning Signs: Tales of Horror and Dark Fantasy

Tales so mesmerizing and eerie, they will make your imagination soar and your skin crawl.

From misunderstood spirits to encounters with mythical creatures, these twisted tales include run-ins with ghosts, mermaids, werewolves, sorceresses, vampires, murderers, and their victims.

Delve deep into the shadowy, unexplored territories of the imagination with these stories that are sure to frighten and enchant. Just don't ignore...

the warning signs